D1374638

FREDERICA IN FASHION

FREDERICA IN FASHION

Being the Sixth Volume of
The Six Sisters

M. C. Beaton

WINDSOR
PARAGON

First published 1985
by Macdonald & Co (Publishers) Ltd
This Large Print edition published 2013
by AudioGO Ltd
by arrangement with
Constable & Robinson Ltd

Hardcover   ISBN: 978 1 4713 3384 2
Softcover   ISBN: 978 1 4713 3385 9

British Library Cataloguing in Publication Data available

Printed and bound in Great Britain by
TJ International Ltd

For my brother, David Chesney, with love.

Whether the charmer sinner it, or saint it,
If folly grow romantic, I must paint it.
Alexander Pope, 'To a Lady'

CHAPTER ONE

'Dear Minerva,' Frederica Armitage wrote. 'By the time you receive this, I shall be Far Away in a Foreign Country.'

Frederica was shy, dowdy and timid. But family circumstances had caused the worm to turn.

She had decided to run away from the ladies' seminary in which she had passed a sedate year being groomed with all the boring educational arts considered necessary for a young lady of fashion.

The blow of her mother's death had been severe, and almost as severe had been the one delivered by her father, the Reverend Charles Armitage, vicar of the parish of St Charles and St Jude. He had blithely announced his intention of marrying again. Frederica's new 'mama' was to be the young vicarage maid, Sarah Millet—Sarah with her flirty, bouncy ways and her supreme vulgarity.

Had Frederica been as beautiful as her five sisters, the famous Armitage girls, then she might have borne her lot with better fortitude, knowing that marriage would provide an escape from her home after her first Season. But Frederica was the youngest and sadly plain. Her early promise of beauty had faded. Her dark curls had changed to faded wispy locks of an indeterminate colour. Her eyes seemed to have no colour at all. Sometimes they looked blue, sometimes green, sometimes grey, but most of the time—just colourless.

She was very small for her seventeen years, only just above five feet high. Her figure was slight and her ankles neat, but her bosom was disappointingly

1

small.

Her sisters had all made stunningly successful marriages; Minerva, the eldest, had married Lord Sylvester Comfrey. After her, Annabelle had married the Marquess of Brabington; then Deirdre, Lord Harry Desire; Daphne, the rich Mr Garfield; and, a month ago, Diana had married Lord Mark Dantrey.

Frederica dreaded the idea of a Season in London. She had nightmares about sitting in hot ballrooms, propping up the wall.

But more than anything else did she dread the idea of having Sarah Millet for a stepmama. Frederica's term at the seminary was to finish in a month's time. Her father had written to say that Sarah would arrive on that day to escort her home. It was not the fact that Sarah was a mere vicarage maid that dismayed Frederica—it was Sarah herself: Sarah, with her bold, wandering eye and cackling laugh.

Frederica had sadly decided flight was the only answer. She had some money saved from the generous gifts sent her by her sisters. But she knew that would not last forever. She would have to find a job. She knew she was far too young to find a post as a governess. She would need to find work as a servant.

After some hard thought, Frederica had determined it was not the rank or position of servant that mattered, it was the standing and nature of the employer.

It would need to be some establishment far enough away from the school to escape notice, but not too far. It would also need to be a place with a very large staff where she would have less chance of being noticed, one of those large mansions which were like small villages.

From gossip in the seminary, she had learned that the Duke of Pembury's country seat was some ten miles distant. Maria McLellan, one of the pupils, had been there with her parents on the day of the duke's annual fete and had said the servants were as well-dressed and well-fed as fine ladies and gentlemen.

But in order to gain employ in any household, let alone a ducal one, references were needed. With great ingenuity, Frederica had set about forging two. She wrote one letter purporting to come from a Mrs. Betwynd-Pargeter which said that Miss Sarah Millet—Frederica had decided it would be a nicely ironical touch to use Sarah's name—was a neat and exemplary sort of person who had started work as a kitchen maid, and, by dint of hard work, diligence, and honesty, been appointed to the position of chambermaid. The second letter, from a Mrs Hamworth, lauded the praises of this chambermaid-extraordinary. Frederica had decided the post of chambermaid would not be too fatiguing or demand too much expertise.

The trouble was that she dare not write from the seminary, applying for a post. She would need to escape from the school and turn up at the duke's kitchen door with her letters, and leave the rest to fate.

The last letter she had to write was the hardest one of all. She could not bear the thought of her family worrying themselves ill over her disappearance, and so, after much thought, she decided to write to her eldest sister, Minerva.

After the first sentence, Frederica put down the

quill and rested her little pointed chin on her hands and thought wistfully of a magical foreign country full of sunshine and gaudy parrots, palm trees, and blue seas, a country that had never heard the name Sarah Millet, and where she, Frederica, would be hailed as a great beauty. She sighed and dipped the quill into the ink well on the standish and continued her letter. 'I feel since there is no hope of my securing an Eligible Parti due to a sad lack of looks, a Season would be a deal of unnecessary expense. I cannot, dear Minerva, countenance the thought of having Sarah Millet as a stepmother. I fear she does not love Papa, but is merely Using him for her own Sinister Ends.' Sinister Ends' seemed rather strong, but in the novels which Frederica loved to read, people were always using other people for their Sinister Ends. 'Therefore, I am Running Away. Do not worry about me, but be assured of all my Love and Affection for you and my other Dear Sisters. Yr. Loving Friend and Sister, Frederica.'

A tear blotted the signature. Frederica felt very young and alone. But return to the vicarage with Sarah Millet, she would not!

She sanded the letters. The one to Minerva would be sent off as soon as she left.

Now, to escape.

But was it necessary to do anything so uncomfortable as climb down knotted sheets in the middle of the night?

Frederica picked up the quill again. The next letter she wrote was supposed to have come from her father.

She deftly copied his large, clumsy script and appalling spelling. Addressed to the head of the seminary, Miss Grunton, the fake letter from the

4

vicar asked that his daughter be put in a post-chaise directly and sent home. Miss Grunton could keep the rest of the school fees which had been paid in advance. When the post-chaise arrived, thought Frederica, she would simply direct it to the Duke of Pembury's home. No, that would not do! When her flight was discovered, they would question the driver of the post-chaise and he would tell them she had been taken to Hatton Abbey, the duke's home. Frederica scowled horribly. Then her brow cleared. She would ask the driver to take her to a respectable inn as near as possible to the ducal residence and then dismiss him. That way, she could fortify herself with a good meal before her ordeal.

A letter had arrived that day for Frederica from Squire Radford, her father's friend and neighbour. The squire had merely written a short note giving Frederica the gossip of the village of Hopeworth. But she could tell Miss Grunton that the letter from her father had been enclosed with the squire's.

The seminary was an expensive one, and Frederica had a room of her own. She was able to begin packing her clothes without being observed.

After half an hour of packing, she felt strong enough to go to see Miss Grunton.

Miss Grunton was a tall, thin lady who wore starched caps of an enormous height and stiffness. Her eyes were weak and watery and her nose was long and red. As usual, she smelled of a mixture of bleach, parma violets, and gin.

As Frederica entered, Miss Grunton, with the ease of long practice, neatly deposited a thick, green glass bottle in the flower vase on her desk.

'Miss Armitage,' she said, baring black

5

and yellow teeth. 'You was absent from Miss Chichester's class.'

'I was packing, ma'am,' said Frederica.

'Packing?'

'Yes, ma'am. Here is a letter from my father which was enclosed in the letter to me from Mr Radford. I did not read it, *of course*, since it was addressed to you, but Mr Radford tells me that Papa wants me home immediately.'

Miss Grunton fumbled in the lace at her bosom for her quizzing glass and then studied the letter, her lips moving soundlessly.

'Lawks!' she said finally. 'It is too late to send you today, Miss Armitage.'

'First thing tomorrow will do,' said Frederica.

'Very well. Most odd. My gels never travel without a maid. Perhaps I can send my Lucy.'

'Please do not, ma'am. Lucy has the cold and Papa is frightened of colds.'

'Dear, dear, yes. Well, I will send round to John's Livery and have them come round at nine tomorrow morning. But I will write to your papa, Miss Armitage, a most *stern* letter, telling him this is not a genteel way to go on. Your time is not yet finished, and yet your fees have been paid . . .'

'Perhaps he says something about not wanting any money back?' said Frederica, wondering, not for the first time, whether Miss Grunton were illiterate.

Once more the eye glass came out and the letter came up.

Frederica sighed with a mixture of impatience and guilt as Miss Grunton tried to decipher the letter.

'The light is failing,' said Frederica at last.

'Please let me read it to you.'

'Will you, dear child? How very thoughtful.'

Frederica read the letter, laying emphasis on the bit about the vicar waiving the return of any of the school fees.

'How generous!' said Miss Grunton. 'Of course we must do as he requests. You will want to take leave of your friends, Miss Armitage, so I will allow you to join the other girls.' But Frederica was too shy and retiring to have made any friends, apart from Bessie Bradshaw who had left three months ago, although she was glad to have an excuse to leave the room, relieved that the first part of her plan had worked.

Frederica made her way back upstairs to complete her packing. She then knelt down and said a brief prayer for her dead mother's soul, feeling grief wrenching at her heart. Frederica never quite knew whether she was grieving for her mother or grieving for some dream mother she had never had. Mrs Armitage had been a professional invalid and had died the previous year after overdosing herself with patent medicines. Frederica had never really known her very well since Mrs Armitage had either been in the throes of her latest Spasm or had been sunk into an opium-induced dream.

Miss Grunton announced at supper that night that Miss Armitage was leaving the seminary. Frederica was immediately surrounded by a crowd of twittering, caressing misses. *Dear* Freddie. Quite the *bestest* friend anyone ever had.

Innocent Frederica was moved to tears. She had not realized everyone was so fond of her.

They ran away to their rooms to find little gifts

7

for her. They pressed addresses on her and made her promise to write.

The sad fact was they did not care for Frederica in the slightest—only for the very high standing in London society of Frederica's sisters. Any hopeful debutante could hope to further her marriage career by being on intimate terms with the Armitages. Each had meant to do something about befriending dreary little Frederica before the end of term and all were now scrabbling to make up for lost time.

But naive Frederica was deeply touched and nearly made up her mind to give up the whole idea of the Great Escape. But that would mean forging *more* letters to explain why she was *not* going, and then, when she *did* leave, Sarah Millet would be waiting to take her back to Hopeworth. Hopeworth was the village where the Armitage vicarage stood.

The next eldest of the sisters to Frederica, Diana, had once run away from home dressed as a boy. But Diana, thought Frederica wistfully as she prepared for bed, was an expert huntress and horsewoman. Frederica was secretly afraid of horses and thought hunting was cruel.

Before she fell asleep, she consoled herself with the thought that she could always change her mind, even at the very last minute.

But next morning, and the last minute, came all too soon. Had it been a rainy day then perhaps Frederica might have changed her mind. But the sun was shining brightly, the sky was blue, and a south wind carried all the promise of spring. It was a day for adventure.

Frederica kissed all her brand-new friends goodbye and climbed into the post-chaise promising, yes, she would write.

As soon as the gates of the seminary were closed behind her, she called to the driver to set her down at 'that inn near Hatton Abbey'. She mendaciously added that her father who was to meet her there had given her the name but she had lost it.

'That'll be *The Magpie*,' said the driver, and Frederica quickly agreed.

The horses clopped through the early spring sunshine. The thick hawthorn hedges on both sides of the road were faintly tinged with green. The bright little song of the hedge sparrow trilled through the open window of the carriage. Flowers were already beginning to colour the fields and hedgerows, dandelion, daisy, groundsel, thistle, and hawk-weed.

Frederica leaned her head back and decided to enjoy the drive and forget about her future life as a servant. She imagined instead that she was going home, driven by the vicarage coachman, John Summer. Betty, the former maid, would be waiting at the door, and all her sisters, still unmarried, would be there to greet her and make a fuss over her. The twins, her brothers Peregrine and James, would not be young men at Oxford University, but schoolboys, laughing and joking the way they used to. They would all laugh and gossip and then Minerva would tuck them all up in bed and read them a story.

The vicarage had never really been the same after Minerva left to get married, thought Frederica wistfully. Minerva had been the real 'mother', the one to whom they all had turned. Now Minerva had a husband and children of her own.

Minerva!

9

Frederica sat bolt upright. She had asked Miss Grunton to post that letter to Minerva. What if Minerva did not yet know of their father's proposed marriage? Certainly, the vicar had shown no signs of saying anything about it at Diana's wedding.

She bit her lip. Well, Minerva would need to know about it sooner or later.

But worries came crowding into Frederica's mind. What if she did not get a post in the duke's household? What then?

She thought furiously and then decided to bespeak a room for the night at the inn. She would also, if she secured the job, need to leave behind most of her belongings. She did not want to occasion comment by arriving with a wardrobe of fine gowns. A chambermaid would be expected to have a summer dress and a winter dress, and very little else apart from her uniform, a uniform which Frederica hoped would be supplied. And if she *did* not get the job, then she would have somewhere to stay the night while she planned what to do next.

Most of her clothes were much too pretty anyway, thought Frederica gloomily. She *had* been pretty once, she remembered, but when she was thirteen she had contracted the smallpox, which, although it had left her unmarked, had somehow seemed to fade everything about her—her eyes, her hair, and her personality. Things and people seemed to hurt so much, thought Frederica. And the more they hurt, the more you crept farther back into your shell for fear of being hurt again.

Once, when she was fourteen, she had been shopping in Hopeminster, the county town near Hopeworth, with her mother. A deaf, elderly gentleman had suddenly said in a loud voice to his companion, 'Never tell me that's one of the Armitage gels! She's a homely little thing.'

How *that* had hurt! For weeks and *weeks* it had smarted and burned.

But Frederica's spirits took a mercurial upsurge as she looked around the smiling countryside. She could hardly believe she, of all people, had finally and actually *run away,* the sort of thing only very bold people did. 'So I cannot be so very timid and lifeless,' said Frederica aloud. Her little bosom swelled with pride. Diana was Frederica's heroine. Now she was behaving as bravely as Diana!

'I shall go on being brave,' said Frederica, still speaking out loud, that habit of the solitary. 'It is such a wonderful feeling.'

She smiled sunnily at the driver of the post-chaise as he helped her down outside *The Magpie,* a wide, enchanting smile which seemed to turn her eyes as blue as the sky above.

'Bless my heart!' thought the driver. 'What a pretty little thing.'

He good-naturedly told miss that she would find *The Magpie* thin of company because it had, until recently, the worst food for miles around and the lumpiest beds. But the new proprietors, Mr and Mrs Gilpin, had made a fair job of bringing it up to scratch, and miss would find everything of the best.

Frederica thanked him and tripped into the inn.

She was well aware that seventeen-year-old misses did not arrive at inns sans maid, sans booking, sans any servant or companion whatsoever. But her pleasure in her own newfound bravery carried her through the necessary lies. Her maid had fallen sick and had to remain behind at the seminary. Yes, her papa would be calling for her on the morrow.

She was shown up to a pretty bedchamber by Mrs Gilpin and promised a cold collation when she came back downstairs. Frederica had already noticed two tables set out in the inn garden which ran down to the edge of a sparkling river. She asked if she might eat her meal out of doors, and then set about looking through her clothes, selecting the plainest items.

When she was eventually found to be missing, they would surely discover this inn and find her clothes. Of course, if she did not pay her shot, then the landlord might sell her clothes to defray the bill and that might hurt Frederica's generous sisters who had presented her with so many of the pretty gowns. Frederica sighed. So many things to think of! She would pay her shot in advance and that would solve the problem.

A chambermaid came into the room to light the fire. Frederica studied her with interest. She was a thin, pale girl with red hair and a freckled face.

Have you worked here for long?' asked Frederica, judging the girl to be about her own age.

The girl bobbed a curtsy. I must remember that, thought Frederica. Always curtsy. 'About five year, miss,' said the maid. 'I started work for the old owners, but they wasn't as nice as Mr and Mrs Gilpin.'

Bad grammar, mused Frederica, is essential. 'And do you work very hard?' she asked.

The chambermaid's eyes shifted uneasily. 'I do me work well, miss.'

'I am sure you do,' said Frederica earnestly. 'But is it very exhausting?'

'Beg parding?'

'I mean, do you get *tired?*'

'All who works gets tired,' said the maid, her mouth beginning to set in a mutinous line. 'Now, if you'll be excusing of me, miss . . .'

She poked her head under the bed, withdrew the chamber pot, and, finding it empty, replaced it.

'Oh, dear,' said Frederica aloud. 'Chamber pots! I had forgotten about *them.*'

The chambermaid eyed her nervously and began to back towards the door.

'Would you be wanting anything else, miss?'

Frederica wanted to ask her all sorts of questions but knew the maid had already decided this young visitor was strange, to say the least, so she shook her head.

After the maid had left, she decided to put on one of her grandest gowns before going downstairs. She would not have a chance to wear anything so fine, ever again.

She put on a white muslin morning gown, and, over it, a white muslin pelisse, opening down the front and ornamented with a deep flounce. Both pelisse and gown were high-waisted. She tied a white chip Gypsy bonnet on her head and then donned lemon kid gloves and shoes.

She did not look in the glass to admire the effect since Frederica always found her reflection sadly disappointing. She merely checked to see that her hat was on straight and that her soft kid gloves were wrinkled up to the elbow in quite the best manner.

After she had paid for her room in advance, she was ushered into the garden by Mrs Gilpin and served with a cold collation.

'It is very quiet here,' said Frederica, sighing with pleasure as she looked about the sunny garden.

13

Mrs Gilpin thought she was talking about the inn. 'It's a quiet time of year, miss,' she said defensively, 'and it's not as if we's on the main London road. Furthermore, this place got such a reputation for bad victuals as never was. Folks are just beginning to find out about us. Why, the Duke of Pembury hisself oft comes here now.'

'What is he like?' asked Frederica. 'The duke, I mean.'

'A fine gentleman. *A real* gentleman. Not like some. And them tattle-tales in the village can call him the Wicked Duke fill they's black i' the face, but it won't change my mind.'

'The Wicked Duke!' said Frederica faintly. 'Why do they call him that?'

'Because they've got more hair than wit. Now, would you be wanting wine or ratafee?'

'Lemonade, please,' said Frederica.

The landlady turned and bustled off.

Frederica's pleasure in the quiet garden had somewhat dimmed. The Wicked Duke. Perhaps he was a dreadful old lecher, but free with his money, which was why Mrs Gilpin would like him. Oh, dear! But low mortals such as chambermaids would have nothing to do with so grand a person as the duke. Her fate would depend more on the temperament of the housekeeper.

Frederica picked up her knife and fork, and decided to eat first and think some more about the problem later.

It was very pleasant in the garden. An old peach tree leaned against a mellow brick wall. The river rippled and chuckled at the foot of the garden and birds were building their nests in the branches high above Frederica's head.

14

'It would be wonderful,' she thought, 'if life could always be like this, pleasant and warm and secure.'

Then the peace was disturbed by the rumble of arriving carriage wheels. Frederica hoped the new arrival or arrivals would not join her in the garden.

Then, 'In the garden, I think,' came a deep voice, and just as Frederica was recovering from a twinge of annoyance because her solitude was going to be disturbed, Mr Gilpin's answering voice said, 'Certainly, your grace. There is a school miss in the garden, but I'll tell her to move.'

'That will not be necessary,' answered the deep voice.

The duke! The Duke of Pembury! Frederica wished she had put on a poke bonnet instead of the frivolous Gypsy affair which did not conceal one bit of her face.

She dropped her knife and fork and half made to rise, her food barely touched, when that deep voice said right behind her, 'Pray be seated. You do not need to stand.'

Frederica blushed and sat down without looking around. The duke obviously thought she had jumped to her feet out of deference to his rank.

All her usual timidity came flooding back like the tide of red suffusing her face. Her knees trembled and she felt quite sick.

But it was so awful to revert to shy, frightened Frederica again, just when she had been enjoying the novelty of being brave and adventurous. Only look at the way she had so boldly demanded to have her meal served in the garden . . . well, *requested*. She straightened her spine and resolutely picked up her knife and fork.

She was intensely aware of the tall figure sitting

15

at the other table, a little way away, although she could not bring herself to look at him direct.

Then the full staff of the inn appeared in the garden, laying the cover for his grace, bowing before his grace, offering his grace wine, offering his grace every kind of delicacy that the inn had to offer.

'I wasn't offered a choice of *anything*,' thought Frederic; and the cold collation, which had looked so appetizing, now looked dull and tired.

She decided to assert herself, and, pushing the lemonade a little away, she said in a loud voice, 'I would like some wine. Canary, if you please.'

'In a minute, miss,' said Mrs Gilpin.

'I would like some wine now,' said Frederica, feeling she was behaving very badly indeed, and at the same time enjoying the novelty.

Mrs Gilpin muttered something and hurried off. Soon a decanter of canary was put in front of Frederica along with a clean glass. Mrs Gilpin hurriedly poured out some wine for Frederica and then rushed off to attend to the more important customer.

Frederica had still not looked at the duke.

She kept her face slightly averted for she did not want the duke to see her too clearly in case he might recognize her later.

The duke was finally served and Mr and Mrs Gilpin and their servants withdrew.

Silence fell again on the pretty garden. Shadows of new leaves moved across the grass and a thrush sang his repetitive serenade to spring. The warm air smelled of newly cut grass, woodsmoke, roasting meat and wine.

Frederica had firmly decided to quell any

overture from the duke, should he try to speak to her.

But he did not.

As the wine in Frederica's decanter sank lower, so did her spirits grow bolder.

She began to feel piqued that this duke had not even bothered to say good day.

She turned and looked at him fully for the first time.

CHAPTER TWO

There was a long silence while the ill-assorted pair studied each other.

Frederica thought the title of the Wicked Duke suited her companion very well.

He had thick, black hair worn longer than the usual fashion. His eyebrows were very thin, black and arched over jet-black eyes with curved eyelids. His face was very white and high-nosed and his mouth was firm and rather cruel.

He was well above the normal height with broad shoulders. His blue morning coat had a black velvet collar, his long waistcoat was black, as were his breeches and top boots. His hands were long and white and a large ruby ring blazed on the middle finger of his left hand.

But it was not his appearance alone that made him look so satanic. It was the air of cruelty mixed with arrogance that seemed to emanate from him.

The duke saw a rather colourless schoolgirl in a very modish gown and pelisse. He noticed her take stock of him and then saw the slight smile of distaste that curled her pink mouth.

'I' faith, Miss Whatever-Your-Name-Is,' he said, 'I do hope your curiosity is satisfied, for I am not in the way of being stared at like some two-headed freak at Bartholomew Fair.'

'I beg your pardon, sir,' said Frederica, quickly turning her head away.

She knew she had been very rude to stare at him like the veriest yokel, but she really never had seen anyone quite like him before. Her brothers-in-law were all imposing men, but not one of them seemed so devilish as this duke.

She picked up her knife and fork again, determined to finish her food as quickly as possible and make her escape.

But, at that moment, Mrs Gilpin and two waiters came into the garden, bearing the duke's meal.

For once, Frederica blessed her colourless appearance. The duke would not recognize her if he saw her in his household as a servant.

The garden was again quiet. She gave a little sigh and bent to pick up her reticule.

'It is a pleasant day, is it not?' said the duke.

Frederica pretended not to hear. She no longer wanted to find herself engaged in conversation with someone who, she hoped, was to be her future employer.

'Are you deaf as well as insolent?' demanded the duke.

Throwing caution to the winds, Frederica turned and faced him.

'I was not aware you were speaking to me, sir,' she said coldly. 'What did you say?'

'It is of no matter. What are you doing, at your age, living unescorted in this out-of-the-way inn?'

18

'Because you are obviously a great deal older than I,' said Frederica primly, 'it does not give you the right to ask me personal questions when we have not even been introduced. But, as a matter of fact, I am waiting for my father. He is to join me here and escort me home.'

'Home being where?'

'Do stop asking questions,' said Frederica crossly.

The Duke of Pembury raised his thin eyebrows. He had never in all his life been so snubbed by any female, young or old:

'My name is Pembury,' he said haughtily.

'Well, Mr Pembury . . .' began Frederica maliciously.

'I am the Duke of Pembury. I own all the land about here.'

'I do not know whether you expect congratulations,' said Frederica, 'but since you probably inherited it all from your father, you were no doubt simply trying to impress me.'

'Impress *you*. My dear girl, I am not in the way of trying to impress anyone.'

'Really? You surprise me.'

The duke glared at her, and then he smiled. 'I have never before met anyone who managed to make me feel quite so pompous or so ancient.'

Good-naturedly, Frederica smiled back, that wide, enchanting smile of hers that lit up her whole face. 'You are not *very* old,' she said in a kind voice.

'I am over thirty.'

'Never mind. You do not show your years *at all*, I assure you.'

'Thank you,' he said dryly. 'You have not told me your name.'

19

'Miss Frederica Armitage.'

'Armitage? Not the famous Hopeworth Armitages?'

'No,' lied Frederica. 'Hopeminster. But I am not related to the Hopeworth Armitages.'

'I thought not.'

'No,' said Frederica's canary-wine-loosened tongue pertly. 'I am not pretty enough.'

'I did not say so.'

'But you thought it.'

'Odd's fish, girl, did that seminary of yours not teach you to put a curb on your unruly tongue?'

Frederica flushed slightly. 'I think I have had rather too much wine to drink,' she said candidly. 'I am not in the way of drinking wine.'

He studied her curiously and found himself wondering about the colour of her eyes. A moment before, when she had smiled, they had seemed blue, then, when she was angry or upset, they turned a silvery colour. Most odd.

'Do you have many servants?' she asked.

'Yes.'

'Are you a good master?'

'I employ good masters. I make a point of seeing that my servants are well-fed and well-dressed.'

'Do you like them? Your servants?'

'*Like* them?' Again the thin eyebrows went up. 'My dear child, I do not hire help or have help hired because of charm or popularity. A man or woman must be neat, unobtrusive, and hard-working.'

'Why are you called the Wicked Duke?'

'Because of the follies of my youth. I was very wild.'

'And now you are reformed?' Frederica sounded a shade disappointed.

'No, merely staid and old, Miss Armitage. Pray drink some lemonade and leave that wine alone or goodness knows what you will ask me next.'

'Are you much at home?' pursued Frederica, pushing away the wine decanter and dutifully filling a glass with lemonade.

He smiled. 'No, I travel a great deal. I shall shortly be leaving for London to be there when the Season begins.'

'Why?'

'That is quite enough I have indulged you sufficiently. Oh, dear, how oddly you look at me. I am looking for a wife, and a wife is usually to be found at the Season.'

But there are ladies everywhere.'

'None, perhaps, suitable to my rank.'

'Surely character and . . . and . . . a pleasing manner, and honesty . . . and . . . and oh, humour and things like that are of more importance than rank.'

'I have a very large establishment. The lady I marry would need to be a good hostess, witty, well-dressed, and amusing.'

Frederica fell silent.

She felt she ought to leave. She obscurely felt this sinister-looking duke was dangerous. But she was aware of his gaze on her and she felt too self-conscious to rise from the table.

'And you, Miss Armitage,' came his voice, 'do you plan to visit London this Season?'

'No, I shall be employed . . . elsewhere.'

'But you do plan to marry?'

'No, your grace.'

'Your parents have need of you at home?'

'No, your grace. My mother is dead and my

21

father has servants enough.'

'You do not like men?'

'I fear, your grace, I have decided that gentlemen do not like me. I am not well-favoured.'

'Stuff,' he snapped. 'You have all the makings. You have simply not yet learned how to use them.'

All at once appalled at the intimacy of the conversation and sobered by fresh air and lemonade, Frederica rose to her feet. He punctiliously stood up, his tall figure looming over her in the sunny garden.

'Forgive me,' said Frederica. 'I must leave.' He bowed.

Frederica swept him a low curtsy. Frederica's curtsies were a miracle of grace and deportment, and one of her many social talents.

The duke stood watching her as she left the garden. He had a sudden impulse to call her back. The strange colourless little thing had enlivened the tedium of his existence. It would have been amusing to make her smile again, and see how that enchanting smile of hers turned her briefly from a plain school miss into something beautiful and elusive.

He sat down again, reminding himself that he had already behaved far out of character by talking to her for so long.

Frederica retired to her room and sat for a long time, deep in thought. She would stay the night at the inn, and travel to Hatton Abbey in the morning. It was as well that great personages such as dukes did not employ their servants themselves.

The Duke of Pembury finished his meal in the garden and then called for his carriage.

He recollected with some irritation that he had

22

invited a great number of guests who were all due to arrive at the end of the week, and that, for once, he had forgotten to warn his staff.

When he arrived at Hatton Abbey, he promptly sent for his butler, Mr Anderson, his housekeeper, Mrs Bradley, and his groom of the chambers, Mr Smiles.

He informed them of the forthcoming house party, looking at their expressionless faces and wondering for the first time what they thought But his well-trained servants merely murmured woodenly, 'Yes, your grace. Certainly, your grace.'

'If you need more staff, hire local people,' said the duke, dismissing them.

He sat down at his desk and ran through the guest list which his deferential secretary had laid in front of him.

'Lady Godolphin,' said the duke, twisting about and staring at his secretary. 'Why is that Mrs Malaprop, that old rip, included? I do not recall inviting her.'

'I beg to remind your grace,' said his secretary, Mr Hugh Grant, 'that Lady Godolphin invited you to supper a year ago, an invitation which you accepted. You told me to return the hospitality only when there was to be a large number of other guests present since you did not think you could bear much of her ladyship's company undiluted. I thought this house party would be an excellent occasion.'

'Very well, I suppose you have the right of it. Lady Caroline James. My dear Grant. My dear, *dear* Grant. That is yesterday's mutton you are serving.'

'I invited Lady James on your instructions,' said

23

Mr Grant plaintively. He was a chubby young man, very much in awe of his master. 'I did not know the situation had changed. You did not inform me of any change, your grace.'

The duke scowled. 'I am sure . . . never mind, Mr Grant. I am surprised she accepted the invitation.'

Lady James was his ex-mistress. She had taken her dismissal with her usual sophisticated ease of manner and he had given her a very generous settlement.

He would have thought, however, that the experienced Lady James would have realized his secretary must have made a mistake.

He ticked off the other names, and, as he did so, he found his thoughts wandering back to that odd little girl at the inn. Perhaps he might send a servant over in the morning to find out if her father had arrived. Such a young lady should not be left to her own devices, especially since she had shown an alarming tendency to drink too much and become over-familiar with strangers

Then he shrugged. Miss Armitage appeared well able, nonetheless, to look after herself. And it was highly unlikely he would ever see her again.

*   *   *

The next day, Frederica Armitage, leaving behind her trunks, except for one small one containing two dresses and two pairs of plain shoes and some underwear, set out from the inn.

She was wearing a plain grey gown with a black spencer. She had taken the flowers and ribbons off one of her oldest straw bonnets and crushed it into a suitably meek and unmodish shape.

24

The weather had turned grey and overcast. Frederica did not ask for directions to Hatton Abbey until she had walked several miles from the inn.

She was relieved to find that she had only two more miles to walk until she came to the west lodge, for the sky was growing blacker and the wind was rising.

Her courage was beginning to fail, dropping from her shoulders like a cloak. But the thought of the miles she would have to trudge back to the inn if she changed her mind, and of how she would chastise herself for her lack of spirit, drove her on.

At last she reached the west lodge. An elderly lodge keeper came out and looked at her suspiciously through the tall iron gates.

Frederica took a deep breath and dropped him a curtsy.

'I've come about a job, sir,' she said.

'Expecting you, is they?' demanded the lodge keeper.

'Yes, sir,' said Frederica meekly.

'Well, come through the little gate at the side. Don't expect me to open they gurt gates for you.'

Frederica saw a little gate at the side of the great crested iron ones and let herself through.

She could feel the eyes of the lodge keeper boring suspiciously into her back as she walked up the drive, her trunk banging against her legs.

The drive seemed even longer than the walk from the inn. It ran through fields where cattle grazed, then tall, dark woods where deer flitted silently through the trees, and then finally arrived at acres of green lawn which stretched forward to the abbey walls.

25

Frederica gulped when she saw Hatton Abbey. Her sisters all had grand country houses, Minerva's in-laws lived in a huge place, but never had she seen such a formidable place as Hatton Abbey.

The south front was baroque but the west front was Gothic. Frederica was to discover later that the east was classical and the north, Tudor. But the mixture of architectural styles added to, rather than detracted from, the magnificence of the building.

The drive was ornamented on both sides with tall marble statues on plinths. The gleaming white gigantic figures formed a strange sort of guard of honour for the small figure of Frederica as she walked between them under the darkening sky, dragging her trunk.

By the time she had reached the Abbey, she had forgotten that servants do not enter by the main door.

The door stood open and so she walked into the hall. The hall was a miracle of stone, wood and marble. Paintings, tapestries, carved wood and a painted ceiling made Frederica stare in awe.

Mr Anderson, the butler, emerged into the hall from the nether regions. He scrutinized the small figure standing beside the battered trunk. Despite the shabby hat and lack of maid, his practised eye was not deceived. He recognized expensive dressmaking when he saw it.

'May I be of assistance, miss?' he asked.

Frederica started and looked up into Anderson's face. He was not fat and ponderous like most butlers, but slim, wiry and sallow.

'I am come to ask if you need a chambermaid, sir,' said Frederica.

Anderson's mouth tightened. 'Come with me

26

before anyone sees you,' he scolded. 'Walking in the front door as bold as brass and wearing fine clothes. No better than you should be, probably. We'll see what Mrs Bradley has to say to this.'

Frederica decided she could not go through with it. She half-turned to run when her eye caught the tall figure of the duke emerging from a room at the far end of the hall. With a little gulp, she seized her trunk and followed the butler through a small door and down a steep flight of stairs,

Anderson stopped at a polished wooden door on a half-landing and scratched at the panels.

'Enter,' called a woman's voice.

Anderson strode in, signalling to Frederica to follow him.

The housekeeper, Mrs Bradley, sat in a tapestry covered chair beside the fireplace in her parlour. 'What is this, Mr Anderson?' she demanded. Anderson pushed Frederica forward.

'This baggage comes marching in by the front door, asking for a job as a chambermaid.'

Frederica dropped Mrs Bradley a curtsy and stood with her eyes lowered.

Mrs Bradley was a stout, florid-faced woman encased in black silk. Her large starched cap was surrounded by a starched frill which stuck out all round her fat face. The cap was tied under her chins with two stiff, white, starched ribbons. On the bosom of her gown was pinned a large silver watch, so large it was almost like a clock.

'What have you to say for yourself, girl?' she demanded. She had a surprisingly deep, hoarse voice.

'I came in the hope of employment,' said Frederica.

27

'Ho! And wearing fine clothes. You never bought those duds out of your pay. Stole them, heh?'

'No, ma'am,' said Frederica meekly. 'My late mistress, Mrs Betwynd-Pargeter, give them to me.'

'And why are you not still with this Mrs Betwynd-Pargeter?'

''Cos she died, ma'am. But she give me a reference on her . . . 'er . . . deathbed,' said Frederica, desperately trying to speak like a chambermaid. 'I have two references with me.'

'Let me turn her out,' said Anderson. 'Bold minx.'

'It happens I need a chambermaid what with all these guests his grace has sprung on me, and I would like to remind you, Mr Anderson, that I am quite capable of making up my own mind when it comes to hiring girls.'

Anderson shrugged. 'Don't blame me if she steals the silver,' he said, slamming his way crossly out of the housekeeper's parlour.

'Let me see your references,' said Mrs Bradley.

Frederica fumbled in her reticule and produced the two forged letters. Mrs Bradley lumbered to her feet and searched in a drawer and then produced a small pair of steel-framed spectacles which she popped on her nose.

After studying them, the housekeeper heaved her large bulk back into her chair and peered at Frederica over the top of her spectacles.

'Now, miss, in the normal way I would not engage a girl until I had written to the lady here who is still alive. But I'm sore pressed for staff, and then, it stands to reason that a chambermaid would not have the learning to write these letters herself. Sit down opposite me.'

28

Frederica curtsied again and sat down, her hands folded on her lap and her eyes meekly on the floor.

'You will work with Mary, and will be given the guest ladies' bedrooms in the East Wing. If you become permanently employed then you will be given two bolts of cloth for to make dresses, two print and two black.

'Did your former employers engage many servants?'

'No, ma'am, nothing compared with the great number you must have here,' said Frederica.

'Your duties may not seem quite so hard as those you have been accustomed to, because we do employ a great many persons. But mark you, *no* skimping. You always take a pail of boiling water up to them bedchambers, and after you empty the chamber pots into the slop pail, you scald them out with boiling water and then polish them with a cloth. You must wear a bed apron so that any dirt from your dress won't get on the linen. The beds should be stripped down every day and left for about an hour to air. Now, what's your family?'

'Dead, ma'am,' said Frederica, mentally sending all the fictitious Millets to the grave. 'I was taken on from the orphanage.'

'Well, Sarah Millet, this is your home now, if you're a good girl. You look clean and that's a mercy. How come you speak so ladylike?'

'I copied mistress's voice,' said Frederica-Sarah, although she was surprised at Mrs Bradley's question. She thought she had been speaking very like a chambermaid.

'That's as may be,' growled Mrs Bradley in her hoarse voice, 'but don't go putting on airs above your station. Now, you can join me in a glass of gin

29

and hot, and then I'll introduce you to Mary.

'Mr Smiles is the groom of the chambers. Always call him "sir". If he's dissatisfied with your work and says you must go, then there's nothing I can do to stop him. He's The Law.'

Frederica wanted to ask about wages, but had not the courage. And wasn't she to have any days off?

Mrs Bradley lumbered to her feet again and took a steaming kettle from the hob on the hearth. She poured two half-glasses of gin and topped them up with boiling water.

'King George and the Duke of Pembury?' said Mrs Bradley, tossing the mixture straight down her throat.

'King George and the Duke of Pembury!' echoed Frederica, and poured her glass of gin and hot water straight down her throat as well. Tears started to her eyes as the mixture burned her mouth.

'Goodness,' thought Frederica, 'any more of these toasts and I shall be as hoarse as Mrs Bradley.'

'Now,' said Mrs Bradley, 'pick up your bag and I'll take you to Mr Smiles.'

*   *   *

Minerva, the eldest of the Armitage girls, had just presented her husband, Lord Sylvester Comfrey, with a baby girl.

Unlike the births of the previous two babies, both boys, this one had been difficult. Lord Sylvester would normally never have dreamed of reading his wife's letters, but when he saw the schoolgirlish scrawl that was Frederica's lying among the morning post, he decided to read it.

The Armitage girls were always in some kind of trouble and Minerva always seemed to become involved in it.

He was determined that nothing should disturb his beautiful wife's recovery, and so, after only a little hesitation, he broke the seal and opened the letter.

'The old fool!' he said savagely, meaning the vicar, his father-in-law. If Frederica had run away —although he believed she was romanticizing— then she must be found as soon as possible. This bad news must be kept from his wife.

He went upstairs and quietly entered his wife's bedroom. She had been asleep but awoke as he walked into the room.

She looked so frail that his heart missed a beat. He kissed her gently on the cheek. 'How are you, sweeting?'

'Tired'—Minerva smiled—'but so much better.'

'I am going down to Hopeworth for a few days. There is a new system of land drainage that might interest your father.'

'I think you give Papa *too* much help,' said Minerva. 'He is only interested in hunting, and if you give him money he does not put it into land but simply buys more horses and hounds.'

'We will see. I have managed to persuade him before this to do something about his land.'

'Will you be gone long, Sylvester?' asked Minerva, her grey eyes looking enormous in her pale face. He smoothed her hair back from her brow with a gentle hand.

'No, my love, only a few days. You know I can

31

never leave you for long.'

'You never leave me at all except when there is an emergency. Sylvester . . .' Minerva struggled up against the pillows.

'No. No,' he said soothingly. 'I have some business in Hopeminster in any case. You must admit you have been worried about your father since Diana's wedding when he behaved most oddly. I am sure you would feel better if you knew all was well.'

Minerva looked at him anxiously. She thought she would never know what went on behind his enigmatic green eyes and handsome face.

'You are worrying that I am keeping something from you,' he said. 'But you are quite wrong. I might also call at the seminary and take little Frederica a gift.'

Minerva's face brightened. 'Poor Freddie,' she said. 'We have sadly neglected her. Oh, Sylvester, why do you not bring her here with you? I will be well enough, by the time the Season begins, to chaperone her. Annabelle says she met a very charming captain at the Ruthfords' the other night who would make Freddie a perfect husband.'

'What a match-maker you have become.' Her husband laughed. 'I will try to bring Freddie back with me. She will be company for you. Now, try to sleep. And do not worry. There is nothing the matter. Nothing the matter at all.'

CHAPTER THREE

Once upon a time, the staff at the Hopeworth vicarage had seemed much too small to cater for six girls and two boys as well as the Reverend and Mrs Charles Armitage.

Now they found time lay heavy on their hands, for there was only the vicar to look after. To see to his needs was John Summer, his coachman-cum-groom-cum-kennel master-cum-whipper in. Then there was the odd-man, Harry Tring, who still acted as footman or butler, depending on the importance of the callers. The knife boy was a new one, Herbert, from the Hopeminster orphanage. Cook-housekeeper Mrs Hammer held sway above and below stairs. There was even Rose, a parlourmaid.

And there was Sarah Millet.

Sarah's duties were supposed to be those of lady's maid, but without any ladies in the household, her work had sunk to that of general maid.

And what sort of life was that? thought Sarah grumpily as she walked along by the village pond. Mr Armitage had said he could not announce their engagement to anyone, not until a decent period of mourning for his wife was over. But Diana Armitage had been married a month ago in half-mourning and her father did not seem to see anything wrong with that. 'In a little, Sarah,' he would say. 'Be patient.'

It had been easy to be patient during the dark winter days where there was little else to do but dream of being a fine lady. But spring had come, a warm, caressing spring, reminding Sarah she was a young and pretty girl who had allowed a middle-aged vicar space in her bed—space for which he was becoming increasingly reluctant to pay any rent in the way of marriage.

He had not even allowed her to tell the other servants of her forthcoming marriage, with the result that Mrs Hammer treated Sarah as if she were a slut.

'Which I am not!' thought Sarah fiercely, tossing her head and throwing a saucy glance at a strange young man who was walking towards her.

The gentleman swept off his hat and gave Sarah an appreciative smile. Sarah dropped a demure curtsy and glanced up at the stranger under her long curling lashes.

He was tall, and bronzed as if he had come from foreign parts. He had a quantity of light brown hair, was fashionably dressed, and had a pleasant, handsome face.

'That's a sight I never thought to see again,' he said, 'a pretty English maid walking along on a fine English morning.'

'Have you come from far away?' asked Sarah.

'Yes, my chuck. From America.'

'And do you come from Hopeworth, sir?'

'I am Lady Wentwater's nephew, Guy Wentwater. And where do you live, my fairest?'

'At the vicarage,' said Sarah, with a petulant jerk of her head in that direction.

To her amazement, venom blazed for a moment in Mr Wentwater's eyes. Then he said, 'Pray do not mention my name. I do not like Mr Armitage.'

He bowed and walked on, leaving Sarah looking after him.

Wentwater. Sarah racked her brains Lady Wentwater had not been seen for a long while. Her mansion at the other end of the village had been leased for a short time to strangers, but last winter it had stood empty. It was known in the village, for it had been in all the papers, that Guy Wentwater had left for America after killing a murderer, so that meant he was a brave man. But she had heard hints and mutterings about the vicarage which seemed to indicate he was some sort of villain. He was courting Miss Emily, Sir Edwin Armitage's daughter, and it was well known that she had waited faithfully for his return. Sir Edwin Armitage was the vicar's brother.

Of course, thought Sarah, poor Emily couldn't do else but wait what with a face like hers.

Sarah leaned over the pond, trying to get a glimpse of her reflection in the still water, but all she succeeded in seeing was the top of her fair head and the ribbons on her cap.

She walked on, thinking about Mr Wentwater. Once she was married to the vicar, she would have a chance to meet fine gentlemen like that on an equal level and maybe indulge in something a little warmer.

'Day-dreaming, Sarah?'

Sarah turned slowly round and looked into the boot-button eyes of the vicar of St Charles and St Jude, the Reverend Charles Armitage.

He was a squat John Bull of a man wearing a shovel hat and pepper-and-salt coat. He smelled of damp dog and brandy. Mr Wentwater had smelled of Joppa soap and lavender water.

Sarah's eyes narrowed into slits. 'When are we going to announce our engagement, Charlie?' she said in a loud voice.

The vicar winced. 'Thought we might do it after I get Frederica puffed off.'

'What! She's the plain one. Nobody'll want to many her for ages. You listen to me, Charlie. I've had enough o' old Mrs Hammer's sneers, and when I'm Mrs Armitage, I want her sacked.'

'See here, girl,' growled the vicar, 'if you go on like that, I'll never marry you. Me get rid o' Mrs Hammer! Tish!'

'Well, you can keep your fat hands to yourself and keep out of my bedroom until after the wedding,' said Sarah, standing with her hands on her hips.

The vicar eyed her gloomily from her head of golden curls shining under the frivolous cap to her cheeky, thrusting bosom. 'Take care I don't change my mind.'

'You can't,' said Sarah triumphantly. 'I'll sue you for breach o' promise Besides you told Frederica and stands to reason she'll have told Minerva.'

'Lady Sylvester and Miss Frederica to you,' snarled the vicar. 'Women! You're all a poxy lot.'

'Oooh!' Sarah drew back her plump fist and gave him such a resounding box on the ear that his hat sailed off and fell in the pond.

She marched off down the road, her curls bouncing. 'Jade!' the vicar yelled after her.

A drake was nibbling at his hat and he cursed it roundly. Sometimes the vicar thought the whole of nature was in a plot to conspire against him. There was the old dog fox which had led him such a merry chase over the past few years. He often thought the animal was laughing at him. And now there was that there drake, nibbling at his hat and fixing him

36

with one insolent golden eye.

He heard a step behind him and swung round. Mr Pettifor, his over-worked curate, was standing behind him, open-mouthed.

'Don't just stand there,' said the vicar, 'Get my hat.'

Mr Pettifor hitched up his cassock and looked nervously at the water. Growing tired of the hat, the drake bobbed his sleek head under the water and the resultant little wave sent the hat slowly spinning towards the shore.

Mr Pettifor leaned forward a long arm and fished it out. 'Lord Sylvester says he only intends to stay for one night,' said Mr Pettifor conversationally, handing the vicar his hat.

'What! Comfrey here? Why didn't you tell me?'

'You didn't give me a chance,' said Mr Pettifor plaintively. 'Besides, I thought you knew.'

Seizing his sopping hat, the vicar strode off down the road

He crashed into the vicarage parlour and surveyed his elegant son-in-law. 'How's Merva?' he asked, handing Rose, the parlourmaid, his wrecked hat. 'Fetch us some brandy, Rose.'

'Minerva is not in the best of health,' said Lord Sylvester, fastidiously removing a dog hair from his impeccable pantaloons. 'I wrote to you informing you of the birth of our daughter. Minerva is still weak and needs rest.'

'Unlike you to leave her,' said the vicar, seizing the brandy bottle, pouring two glasses, and tossing off his own before Lord Sylvester had time even to raise his to his mouth.

'No,' said Lord Sylvester equably, 'only another Armitage crisis would drive me from her side.'

'No crisis that I know of,' said the vicar, beginning to relax as the brandy warmed his stomach.

'It seems you have precipitated one. I am not in the habit of reading my wife's post, but I read this one from Frederica because, for some reason, I felt there might be trouble from that quarter.'

He handed over the letter, which the vicar read with increasing wrath and dismay.

He shot his son-in-law a furtive, angry look. The vicar felt trapped. He did not spare much thought to his youngest daughter. He was sure Frederica was merely trying to frighten him. But that she should have told Minerva about Sarah! He had been extremely grateful to Sarah for her favours. But he was gradually becoming accustomed to being single again. Not that the late Mrs Armitage had taken up much of his time, but she had been his wife, and very much what the vicar considered a wife should be . . . genteel, ailing and perpetually complaining. The fact that his handsome daughters did not fit this picture did not alter the vicar's opinion of married women. His daughters were his daughters, and he had never really quite grasped the fact that they were married, even with one of his sons-in-law sitting facing him.

'Is Sarah the one who brought the brandy?' asked Lord Sylvester, remembering vaguely that the Sarah of Frederica's letter was a servant at the vicarage.

'Not her,' said the vicar with some pride. 'Sarah's the pretty one.'

'Worse than I thought,' drawled Lord Sylvester, stretching one booted foot out to the fire.

'And what does that mean?' growled the vicar.

'Simply, the pretty ones are harder to get rid of. They know their worth.'

'Who said anything about gettin' rid o' Sarah?'

'Then you *are* going to marry her?'

'Of course,' said the vicar stoutly.

Lord Sylvester straightened up. 'Then may I suggest you allow the girl to come and reside with one of us until the wedding? You cannot have an affair with a servant girl in a country vicarage and you a vicar. It's a wonder no one from the church, your bishop or archdeacon, has been hammering on the door to excommunicate you.'

'Who said I'd bedded her,' said the vicar sulkily.

'If the whole village is not saying so by now, it's a miracle. And what of your other servants? How does Mrs Hammer feel—giving orders to a maid she knows will shortly be her mistress?'

'Well, she don't know, do she?'

'Worse and worse. You will need to make an honest woman of Sarah as soon as possible.'

'Who do you think you are?' raged the vicar who was secretly afraid of his elegant son-in-law, and like most people, usually hid his fright behind a barrier of anger.

'I am your daughter's husband. I am damned if Minerva is going to be upset by scandal. Now Frederica has threatened to run away. I suggest we both travel to the seminary. If she is still—God willing—there, which I am sure she must be.

'Frederica is given to occasional flights of fancy, but she is much too timid to run away. I will take her back to London with me and turn her over to Minerva. Minerva and her sisters are determined to find Frederica a husband this Season.'

'Very well,' said the vicar, getting to his feet.

39

'But before we go,' said Lord Sylvester silkily, 'I think it would be polite to introduce me to your future bride.'

'She ain't here,' said the vicar hurriedly. 'I left her in the village.'

The slamming of the outside door heralded Sarah's angry arrival home. She erupted into the parlour, and stopped short at the sight of Lord Sylvester Comfrey.

'This here's Sarah,' mumbled the vicar, 'so now, let's be off. Look here, Sarah, seems Miss Frederica is worried 'bout something so me and Comfrey's going over to the seminary.'

Lord Sylvester had risen to his feet at Sarah's entrance. He eyed the short figure of the vicar with cynical amusement. 'You have not formally introduced me to your fiancée, Mr Armitage.'

At that interesting moment, Rose opened the parlour door. 'Mr Radford,' she announced, ushering in the squire. Squire Radford was a small, slight, elderly man, wearing an old-fashioned bag-wig and knee breeches. The vicar often thought gloomily that his Maker had put the squire in Hopeworth village to act as his, the vicar's, conscience.

He was determined the squire should not find out about Sarah.

'You've caught us at a bad moment, Jimmy,' said the vicar with a shifty look. 'Fetch my hat, Rose. Frederica's pining a bit, and Comfrey and me's going to see her. So . . .'

'But first, Mr Armitage was just about to introduce me to his fiancée,' said Lord Sylvester.

'My dear Charles!' exclaimed the squire. 'You *are* a dark horse. I had no idea. Who is the lucky

40

lady? Mrs Petworth over in Hopeminster? Mrs Jones in Berley?' The squire racked his brains for the names of eligible widows. 'Mrs . . .'

'No, it's me,' said Sarah crossly.

The squire sat down suddenly.

Lord Sylvester made Sarah his best bow. 'My felicitations to you both, Miss . . .

'Millet,' beamed Sarah, sinking into a low curtsy.

'Oh, dear,' said the squire.

'Spare me,' groaned the Reverend Charles Armitage.

'I am honoured to meet the future Mrs Armitage,' said Lord Sylvester.

'Lawks!' screamed Rose, the parlourmaid, standing open-mouthed in the doorway, holding the vicar's still sodden hat.

'What's to do?' came the voice of Mrs Hammer behind Rose.

'Oh, Mrs Hammer,' wailed Rose. 'Master is going to marry Sarah.'

'Nooo!' shrieked Mrs Hammer. ''Tain't so.'

'I'm off,' yelled the vicar, seizing his sopping hat from Rose's nerveless fingers and cramming it about his ears.

Sarah Millet looked around her with bold, triumphant eyes. She would move into the best bedroom that very night. And the next day she would send a card over to the Wentwater mansion and she would ask that handsome Mr Wentwater to tea.

*   *   *

Frederica found her life at Hatton Abbey quite pleasant. The chambermaid, Mary, with whom

41

she worked was a cheerful country girl. She had a squashed sort of face as if someone had pressed down hard on the top of her head when she was a baby. Her mouth was very long and large and she had unruly masses of coarse brown hair. The other servants were efficient and hard-working. It was a whole separate world belowstairs with a rigid class system all of its own. Lowly female servants such as chambermaids were only allowed in the housekeeper's parlour on the day of their arrival or the day of their dismissal.

The only servant Frederica did not like was Mr Smiles. He was a fat, pompous man, very proud of his livery and his tall staff of office.

He would appear in the rooms where Frederica and Mary were working, don a pair of white kid gloves, and run his fingers carefully along the ledges, looking for dust.

'At least he can't find anything to complain about,' said Frederica to Mary. 'The rooms are spotless.'

'It'll be different when the guests arrive,' said Mary. 'I hear tell there'll be so much work, it's nigh impossible to do it proper. The beds are supposed to be aired in the morning, but how can you air them when the ladies won't get up until the afternoon? Mr Anderson says as how that Lady James what's coming is always picking on us.'

'Who is Lady James?' asked Frederica. She had given up trying to talk like a servant. Now that she was very much part of the staff nobody seemed to notice.

'She's his grace's fancy piece.'

'Oh.' Frederica was deeply shocked and tried hard not to show it. She had almost begun to

42

think of herself as belonging to the servant class and cheerfully listened to all the gossip about her 'betters', but so far no gossip had touched the magnificent and sinister duke who seemed to be held in awe by everyone, including Mr Smiles.

'Of course, we all thought that was over,' said Mary, pummelling a pillow energetically. 'And good riddance. Mr Anderson says as how he'd rather have old Lady Godolphin any day for all her weird ways.'

'Lady Godolphin,' gasped Frederica. 'Lady Godolphin does not come here, does she?'

'Evidently she came once a long time ago and his grace said "never again".'

Frederica heaved a sigh of relief.

'But for some reason he's asked her back. This is to be her room.'

'But his grace cannot . . . I mean, Lady Godolphin is quite *old*.'

'So you know her?'

'She was a friend of my late mistress,' said Frederica, bending over the fireplace and buffing up the grate to hide the tell-tale blush on her cheeks.

'Well, *of course*, the duke don't fancy Lady Godolphin. He likes high-flyers like Lady James.'

'But surely only common women . . . I mean, Lady James has a title.'

'Don't make her respectable, do it? Her late husband was only a "sir". I tell you, I seen quality ladies with no more manners 'n' a pig.'

Frederica thought furiously. Lady Godolphin would recognize her. She had seen her only a month before at Diana's wedding. But there were ways of hiding without actually disappearing. And

Lady Godolphin would not be expecting to see her. When she did, Frederica would merely be another anonymous servant, opening the shutters. But there was Lady Godolphin's lady's maid. Wait a bit. Something had been said at Diana's wedding about Lady Godolphin having a new maid. Yes, that was it! Someone had complimented Lady Godolphin on her looks and she had said her new maid was a paragroin.

'I thought people called his grace the Wicked Duke because he had been wild in his youth,' said Frederica.

'Oh, he was,' said Mary. 'Mr Anderson said the parties he used to have! Cyprians and lightskirts running screaming through the rooms and every rake-helly gentleman from London after them. But then, his grace settled down amazing. He has mistresses, but one after the other, and he don't keep any of them long.'

'That sounds very wicked to me,' said Frederica sadly.

'You're not sweet on his grace yourself?' Mary laughed.

Frederica shook her head. 'Don't be silly, Mary. He's much too old.'

'He's a man in his prime. The way you talk, you'd think him sixty instead o' thirty. Here, give me a hand with this bed. There was a chambermaid here last year and she was nutty about him, ever so spoony she was. Moped around the passages, hoping he'd notice her.'

'And what happened to her?'

'Well, she wasn't doing her work so Mr Smiles sent her packing.'

Frederica felt a pang of sympathy for the

44

lovelorn maid. She had begun to discover how very lucky she had been to find work so quickly.

'The duke's a good master,' said Mary. 'Oh, you must remember, Sarah, that some of the ladies brings their own linen, and if it don't have a monogram on it, it's easy lost, so we embroider a little sort of sign for each lady. As I was saying about the duke, he takes care of everyone. There's new folk at an inn called *The Magpie* a bit away from here but still on the duke's land. Well, he often goes down there to eat so's to encourage trade for the new landlord. That's finished. Come along. We'd best get as much sleep as we can tonight because the guests arrive tomorrow and, after that, there'll be precious little rest.'

But that night Frederica found, she could not sleep. She wished she had brought some of her precious books with her. She tossed and turned on the bed she shared with Mary. Mary moaned and grumbled in her sleep and then turned on her back and began to snore.

The duke had gone visiting and was not expected back until the small hours. Frederica decided to creep down from her attic and borrow a book from the library.

The great house was still and silent as she made her way downstairs, shielding her candle in its flat stick.

Painted eyes stared down at her from portraits on the walls. A jade Buddha seemed to leap at her out of a corner. Frederica wished herself back in bed. The ghost of a man in black was said to haunt the Long Gallery. But she was still enjoying the novelty of being Brave Frederica, and she knew that she would never forgive herself if she turned about and went back to bed.

A gleaming white statue looked as if it were coyly beckoning from a landing. Her candle flame threw weird shadows up to the painted ceiling as she reached the hall. Mrs Bradley had taken her on a tour of the house so that she would know where all the rooms were in case she had to double as a housemaid when the guests arrived.

She quietly opened the door of the library and went inside. Row upon row of books climbed up to the ceiling behind their glass doors.

Frederica let out a squeak of terror as she saw a ghostly face staring at her from the bookshelves, and, after an agonizing moment, realised she was looking at her own reflection, the white of her nightgown, wrapper and night-cap making her seem like a ghost.

Holding her candle high, Frederica saw a pile of books lying on a console table. Quickly, she looked through them. There was Fanny Burney's *Evelina* in two slim volumes. She picked up the first volume and tucked it under her arm.

There was a crash from the great hall outside as the entrance door to the Abbey opened and closed.

Frederica looked wildly about. There was a high-backed chair beside the fire. She blew out her candle, darted behind it, and crouched down.

To her horror, the library door opened and she heard the duke's voice. 'No, Anderson. I am quite capable of looking after myself. Go back to bed.'

The duke walked into the library. Frederica clenched her teeth to stop them from chattering.

There was the scratching of a tinder box and then the sound of crackling sticks. The duke had lit the fire. Then a soft golden glow spread over the room.

46

He had lit two oil lamps which stood on tables on both sides of the fire. A clink of decanter against glass. Oh, dear, he was pouring himself a glass of wine. He would be here for *hours!*

'Whoever it is crouching behind my chair,' said the duke, 'may as well come out now. I can see you reflected in the glass of the bookcases.'.

'Woooo,' wailed Frederica. 'Woooo. Woooo. *Woooooooo!*'

'Don't be silly,' said the duke. 'I do not believe in ghosts.'

Miserably, Frederica got to her feet.

'That's better. Now come round here where I can see you.'

Frederica shuffled round to stand in front of him.

He was attired in severe black evening dress. His face looked hard and wicked above the foaming white cascade of his cravat. One large emerald winked and gleamed among its snowy folds. He was wearing knee breeches and his long muscular legs were encased in white silk stockings with gold clocks.

'Who are you?' he demanded.

'Sarah Millet, chambermaid to your grace,' said Frederica miserably.

'And what are you doing in my library, Sarah Millet, chambermaid?'

'I thought I saw a cobweb on the table over there,' said Frederica wildly, 'so I came to clear it away.'

'Were you going to wipe it off with that book which you are so ineffectually trying to hide under your wrapper?'

'I'm sorry,' whispered Frederica. 'I couldn't

47

sleep.'

'Give me the book.' He held out his hand. Frederica handed it over.

'Ah, yes,' he said. 'The excellent Miss Burney, or Mrs D'Arblay as she is now. I met her once. She was enchanting.'

'May I go now, your grace?' asked Frederica.

'No, you may not. You bear a remarkable resemblance to a seminary miss I met a few days ago. Not only that, your speech is refined and that night attire is of the finest India muslin.'

'I was very lucky in my last post,' said Frederica, coarsening her vowels. 'Missus gave me ever so many things.'

'Including a taste for novels?'

'Yes, your grace, an it please your grace.'

Frederica shivered under his hard stare. The firelight was shining on his face and two little red flames seemed to dance in his black eyes.

'You are little more than a child,' he said, half to himself. 'Off to bed with you, and do not trespass in my library again without my permission. You may take Miss Burney with you.'

'Oh, thank you,' gasped Frederica. She took the book and then picked up her candle.

'Light it,' he said brusquely. Frederica lit the candle at the fire.

'Will . . . will Mr Smiles hear of this, your grace?' she asked.

'Not this time,' he said.

Frederica smiled suddenly, that bewitching, enchanting smile. Then she turned away and flitted from the room, shutting the door quietly behind her.

'So I have a runaway on my hands,' thought the

48

duke gloomily. 'What is her name, I wonder? First Armitage, now Millet. I had better see Smiles in the morning and get her sent home.'

But the next day his guests began to arrive and the duke, for the time being, forgot about Miss Millet-Armitage.

*　　*　　*

'Gone!' exclaimed the Reverend Charles Armitage. 'My Frederica gone? But I did not send any letter.'

'But she showed it to me,' said Miss Grunton. 'She said it was enclosed with one from Mr Radford. I was to hire a po' chaise and send her immediately.'

'You hen-witted female,' raged the vicar. 'Did ye not think to wonder why I should expect mine own daughter to rent a chaise? To leave without a maid?'

'Enough of this,' said Lord Sylvester curtly. 'From where did you rent this chaise, Miss Grunton?'

'John's Livery,' said Miss Grunton. 'I cannot be blamed, my lord. If Miss Armitage has taken to forging letters, she certainly did not learn it here!' She glared venomously at the vicar.

'Come along, Mr Armitage,' said Lord Sylvester. 'We will find where this chaise took her. Did Frederica have any beaux, Miss Grunton?'

'Oh, no, my lord. We do not allow that sort of thing here. We are a very select seminary.'

John's Livery vouchsafed the information that miss had asked to be set down at *The Magpie,* saying as how her father was going to fetch her.

The vicar began to feel more cheerful. Frederica

49

had obviously decided to give them all a fright, and then make her way home.

But at *The Magpie* they learned that Frederica had gone out walking several days before and had not returned. The trunks that she had left behind were brought up from the cellar.

Mr Armitage was by now badly frightened. He also felt guilty. He did not really want to marry Sarah, and now he was trapped and his daughter had been driven into exile like the thingummies.

He sank down on a hard chair in the hall of the inn and burst into tears.

'Come, Mr Armitage,' admonished his son-in-law. 'At least we have evidence that she is alive.' He turned to the landlord, Mr Gilpin. 'Was there any search for her?'

'Yes,' said Mr Gilpin. 'We told parish constable and some o' the men from the village went all about, but no lady had been seen on the roads around here that day. Only a servant girl and an old woman.'

'Did Miss Armitage meet any gentlemen at the inn?'

'No one, my lord. Leastways, only the Duke of Pembury. They were chatting in the garden, like. His grace often comes here.'

'Where does Pembury live? It is quite near here, I think.'

'Hatton Abbey. Down the road a bit.'

'In that case, I think we should call on Pembury.'

Mr Gilpin bristled. 'Don't you go thinking a fine gentleman like his grace would have aught to do with the young lady's disappearance. Why, as fine a man never—'

'Nonetheless, we shall call.'

50

Much to the worried Lord Sylvester's annoyance, his volatile father-in-law sobbed and groaned all the way to Hatton Abbey. He had heard tell of this duke, the vicar wailed. Black as sin. No morals. His Frederica was ruined.

'Pembury was wild in his youth. 'Tis said he has reformed,' said Lord Sylvester repressively. 'All I want to do is find Frederica and get her safely out of whatever mess she is in before Minerva hears of it.'

*　　　*　　　*

Frederica was bone-weary. She had been nervous and excited when she got back to her room and decided to read herself to sleep. Once she had started on the book, she found she could not put it down. So she had read until the candle had guttered out.

Now the bells were ringing, ringing, ringing. The ladies wanted chocolate, the ladies wanted tea, the ladies wanted cans of hot water, the ladies wanted their own linen put on the bed immediately—and Lady James simply wanted to torment.

She complained of this, she complained of that. The water was not hot enough nor the fire large enough.

In all the running up and down stairs, Frederica could only be thankful that the one lady who did not seem to want anything was Lady Godolphin.

The sheer selfishness of the treatment handed out to servants amazed Frederica. These ladies had all brought their personal maids but it seemed that the bell must be rung so that the over-worked chambermaid should climb the stairs to open a

51

window or make up a fire.

'It's a wonder they don't lose the use of their limbs,' thought Frederica as she piled coal on the fire in Lady James's bedchamber.

Lady James was wearing her undress, a scanty petticoat covered with a frilly negligee. She was a buxom blonde who reminded Frederica of Sarah, although where Sarah's movements were sharp and brisk, Lady James's every gesture was slow and languid. But she had the same bold coarseness about her.

'I must have a buffer for my nails,' drawled Lady James. 'Leave the fire alone and go to that Lady Godolphin female and ask her for one.'

Frederica bobbed a curtsy and went out into the passage and along to Lady Godolphin's bedchamber and scratched on the door. She was so tired, she no longer cared whether Lady Godolphin recognized her or not.

'Come in,' called a hoarse voice.

Frederica went into the room.

The shutters were closed and Lady Godolphin's heavy bulldog face seemed to swim in the gloom. Frederica remembered nervously that Lady Godolphin had a very high-handed way with servants.

Frederica gave a little cough.

'An it please your ladyship, Lady James is desirous of borrowing a buffer for her fingernails.'

'She's here, is she?' demanded Lady Godolphin. 'Thought a man of Pembury's taste would have tired of that coarse jade by now. Well, she can't have it. I'm not having anything of mine polited by that whore of Babbyling, and so you may tell her.'

'Very good, my lady.'

Frederica had learned that it was a servant's business to relay messages with as much accuracy as was politely possible.

With a wooden face, she said to Lady James, 'Lady Godolphin refuses to lend you her buffer. Lady Godolphin says you might polite it.'

'I suppose the old Malaprop means pollute. Tell her from me, I made a mistake. I do not wish to handle anything belonging to her. I have no wish to entertain her lice.'

'Very good, my lady.'

Back went Frederica.

'Lady James begs to inform Lady Godolphin that she has made a mistake and wishes nothing belonging to your ladyship as she does not wish to entertain your ladyship's lice.'

'I ain't lousy, but if I were, it's better than having the pox.'

Frederica blinked.

'Well, go and tell her that, girl.'

Back in Lady James's room, Frederica looked at the cornice and said, 'Lady Godolphin's compliments and she is not lousy, but she would nonetheless prefer to have lice than the pox.'

'Tell her from me, if she wonders why that tottering old fool of a Colonel Brian has not led her to the altar yet, it is because he has found a younger piece of mutton.'

Frederica trailed miserably back to Lady Godolphin and relayed the message.

'Follicles!' screamed Lady Godolphin. She seized a large hat pin and marched to the door. 'Follow me, girl,' she said over her shoulder.

Frederica followed the waddling figure of Lady Godolphin.

Lady Godolphin wrenched open the door of Lady James's bedchamber and charged in, holding the gleaming hat pin in her hand. Lady James shot out a foot. Lady Godolphin tripped over it and crashed on to the floor, screaming like a banshee as she went. She twisted about and sank her teeth, or what was left of them, into Lady James's ankle. Now Lady James began to scream and soon the passageway outside was jammed with curious guests and nervous servants.

Then the crowd parted and the tall figure of the Duke of Pembury shouldered his way into the room. 'What is the meaning of this caterwauling?' he snapped.

Lady Godolphin sat up. 'That piece of laced mutton insulted me,' she said, straightening her bright red wig. 'Why don't you send her packing back to Seven Dials where you found her?'

Seven Dials was London's most notorious slum and famous for its prostitutes.

Lady James turned tear-drenched blue eyes to the duke. 'She insulted me and encouraged this servant girl to be impertinent.'

The duke's black eyes surveyed Frederica thoughtfully.

Mr Smiles oiled his way into the centre of the group. 'One of my servants being impertinent? Dear me, we can't have that. Sarah is a new girl on trial. If she has given offence, I shall send her packing.'

'I only carried messages from one to the other,' said Frederica desperately.

'And she's probably a thief too,' sniffed Lady James. 'That's a book she has in her pocket.'

'A *book*,' said Mr Smiles awfully. 'Give it here.'

Frederica pulled out the volume of *Evelina*. Lady James dabbed at her tears with a tiny scrap of cambric. 'Since she obviously cannot read,' she said, 'she no doubt planned to sell it.'

'I lent it to her,' said the duke and Lady Godolphin in unison. Lady Godolphin had risen to her feet and was staring at Frederica.

'You *what*?' demanded Lady James.

'I lent it to her,' said the duke patiently. 'What I want to know is this, Lady James, am I to expect a continuation of this vulgar behaviour during your stay?'

'Here!' said Lady Godolphin, seizing Frederica's arm. 'Out of here, quick. I want a word with you.'

She propelled the bewildered and shaken Frederica through the watching group of guests and servants and did not release her firm grip on her until they were safely in her room.

'Now . . .' said Lady Godolphin, kicking the door shut behind them. 'What is the meaning of all this . . . Frederica Armitage?'

*   *   *

Rose slammed the tea tray down on the table in the parlour and stalked out, her back rigid with disapproval.

'Uppity servants,' said Guy Wentwater languidly.

'Mrs Armitage spoilt them,' said Sarah airily. 'I shall fire them *all*,' she said, raising her voice, 'Just as soon as I am married.'

'Bravo!' Mr Wentwater grinned, leaning back in his chair with his thumbs in his waistcoat and putting one booted foot up on the other. 'When did you say you were to be married?'

55

'After I chaperone Frederica at her come-out,' said Sarah proudly. She was wearing one of Miss Annabelle's old silk gowns, the former Annabelle Armitage, now the Marchioness of Brabington. She felt it became her much better than it ever did Annabelle. Gone was her cap and apron. Sarah Millet was determined never to wear them again.

Guy Wentwater was highly amused. He had heard all the gossip from his own servants. He knew Sarah was a servant herself, and he thought it a fine joke that the vicar actually meant to marry her, diamond of the first water though she might be. He was also amused at the idea of being entertained in the vicar's home, that clergyman who had once driven him out of Berham County. During all his time in America, Mr Wentwater had promised himself revenge. He once had had hopes of marrying Annabelle, but the vicar had effectively stopped that. Then Deirdre Armitage had made a fool of him. Yes, *all* the Armitages had a lot to answer for. This silly maid might supply him with the means.

He sipped the tea Sarah had poured him and made a face. 'Have you nothing stronger, my lovely?' he said.

'Certainly,' said Sarah grandly, ringing the bell. But though she rang and rang, no one answered its summons. All the servants had in fact gone to the church to meet Mr Pettifor, the curate, to hold a council of war.

Sarah eventually went off to the kitchens to find them deserted and so was forced to fetch and serve the brandy herself.

'So it seems we are all alone,' said Mr Wentwater, pouring a generous measure of brandy for Sarah.

Sarah shrugged. 'I hear you are courting Miss Emily up at the Hall,' she said.

'I wouldn't believe all you hear. Now I heard *you* were a servant.'

'Would I be entertaining you in the middle of the afternoon if I were?' countered Sarah.

'I was only funning,' said Mr Wentwater. 'You are much too pretty to be anything other than a lady. Your hands are so soft.'

He took one of Sarah's dimpled little hands in his own and ran his thumb along the palm.

'Don't do that,' said Sarah, giggling and snatching her hand away. 'What if Mr Armitage was to walk in?'

'But he isn't likely to, is he?' said Mr Wentwater in a caressing voice and retrieving the hand again.

As the afternoon wore on and the shadows lengthened and the brandy sank lower in the bottle, Sarah progressed on to Mr Wentwater's lap, and after that, it seemed only natural that he should pick her up in his arms and carry her up to the bedroom upstairs.

Such a wild and energetic episode followed that neither of them heard the footsteps on the stairs and neither of them was even aware anyone had entered the house until the bedroom door burst open.

They were all there—Mr Pettifor, Mrs Hammer, John Summer, Harry Tring, Herbert, the knife boy, Rose, and, worst of all, Miss Emily Armitage, who let out a great shriek and dropped into a swoon.

'You've done it now, girl,' said John Summer with great satisfaction. 'Turn us all off, would you? And you in master's bed wi' master's worst enemy.'

57

Sarah turned her face into the pillow and began to cry.

'Emily,' wheedled Guy Wentwater, 'do not judge by appearances.' But Emily was being helped to her feet by Rose and Mrs Hammer who led her off down the stairs, making clucking noises of sympathy.

Mr Pettifor stood as if turned to stone, an ugly blush staining his thin cheeks.

'Come along, Mr Pettifor, sir,' said John Summer, putting a comforting arm about the curate's shoulders. 'Such sights are not for the likes of you.'

But Mr Pettifor, staring at Sarah's tumbled golden hair and naked bosom, thought he had never seen anything so beautiful in all his life.

CHAPTER FOUR

'And so that is why I decided to run away, Lady Godolphin,' finished Frederica.

'You should never have been sent to that sinnyrammy in the first place,' said Lady Godolphin. 'I don't hold with education for gels.'

'It wasn't precisely anything to do with learning,' said Frederica. 'Just bits of everything. A little bit of Italian, a little bit of music, a little bit of drawing, and so on.'

'A girl should be taught to write her name and that's all,' said Lady Godolphin. 'Well, you can't stay here. I'm not staying under the same roof as that James creature. You'd best come back to London with me. Minerva's poorly after her last

58

and the only reason she's in town is so's to be ready for your come-out. A bit of country air would do her good. The rest of your sisters say they won't be doing the Season. Going to be in the country. Even Annabelle's gone rusty.'

'Rustic?'

'That's what I said. Now, I found them all husbands and I'll find you one.'

'I don't want one,' said Frederica quickly. 'Men are all philanderers.'

'Don't I know it,' said Lady Godolphin gloomily. 'Ah, well, sweet are the uses of amnesia, as the Bard says. We must struggle to find the best. You can't say any of your sisters married a philanthropist.'

But Frederica was thinking of the duke.

'Don't look so sad,' said Lady Godolphin. 'Minerva ain't up to puffing you off, so I'll do it.'

'It is very kind of you, but . . .'

'Of course, you could return to your pa,' said Lady Godolphin with a wicked gleam in her eye.

'No,' said Frederica. 'Can't I just go on working here?'

'Of course not. Pembury wouldn't allow it, for a start.'

Mary came bouncing in. 'Sarah, I mean, Miss Millet, I mean, your pa is below and he's in a taking.'

Frederica turned white. She was afraid of her father's rages.

'Tell the reverend we'll be down as soon as we're ready,' said Lady Godolphin. 'Ring for my maid.'

'You might have told me you was the Quality,' mumbled Mary as Lady Godolphin was swept off to the dressing room by her maid.

'I thought I no longer was,' said Frederica sadly.

'I did not think anyone would find me. My real name is Frederica Armitage. Now I am to go to London and have a Season.'

'Oh!' Mary clasped her work-reddened hands 'I've never seen London. Just think o' the shops and parties and theatres.'

Frederica gave her a watery smile. She had become very fond of Mary.

'I'll take you with me,' said Frederica suddenly. 'I'll make you my lady's maid.'

'I dunno,' said Mary doubtfully. 'I don't know laces or jewellery or French or . . .'

'I could teach you.'

'But her ladyship won't like it.'

'She won't mind,' said Frederica. '*Please,* Mary.'

'If I do,' said Mary severely, 'you'll need to know your place and not be so friendly-like. And you can't go downstairs in your cap and apron. Let me fetch that dress you come in, and while I get you ready, you can tell me how you come to be working here under another name.'

Frederica was made ready in a very short time indeed but it was a full hour before Lady Godolphin considered herself 'finished' enough to go down. She was wearing a red-and-white-striped merino gown, cut low on the bosom and disgracefully short about the ankle. Over her fat shoulders she wore a fine Paisley shawl. Round her neck she wore a rope of pearls, and on her head a turban of gold gauze embellished with two tall osprey feathers

The Duke of Pembury had never really liked Lady Godolphin until that moment when she erupted into his library with Frederica in tow. She blasted the vicar with a long tirade about his loose morals with all the zeal of a Methodist, leaving the poor vicar, who had been about to castigate his daughter, speechless.

At last, Lord Sylvester interrupted her. 'I am anxious to return to my wife, Lady Godolphin. I think it would be best if I took Frederica with me.'

'Minerva ain't up to a Season,' said Lady Godolphin. 'I'll take her myself. She can stay with me until things at that vicarage have been made respectable again.'

'And what do you have to say to that, Freddie?' asked Lord Sylvester. His voice was kind. Apart from his wife, Lord Sylvester liked Frederica the best of all the Armitage sisters.

Frederica turned to Lady Godolphin. 'Can I take Mary with me?'

'Who's Mary?'

'The chambermaid with whom I worked.'

'I have plenty of chambermaids.'

'I wanted to take her as my lady's maid.'

'You can't turn a chambermaid into a lady's maid. My Martha is the *making* of me,' said Lady Godolphin, revolving slowly so that her charms might be viewed to their fullest.

Frederica gulped. 'I could train her. I really could.'

'Well, I ain't paying her wages,' said Lady Godolphin.

'I will,' said Lord Sylvester. 'You may have your maid, Freddie.'

Frederica hurtled across the room, and, reaching up, hugged as much of her brother-in-law as she could. The Duke of Pembury was amused. He wondered what the members of the London *ton* who were so in awe of the formidably elegant Lord

61

Sylvester would think if they could see him at that moment.

When the vicar had arrived with Lord Sylvester demanding his daughter Frederica Armitage, and implying that he, the duke, had abducted her, it had given the duke great pleasure to take the wind out of the vicar's sails by telling him he believed the runaway daughter to be masquerading as a chambermaid in the household.

'Lady Godolphin,' said the duke, 'since Lord Sylvester is anxious to return to his wife and since Mr Armitage has . . . er . . . affairs to deal with at home, why do you not stay here with Miss Armitage? My guests will only be with me for two weeks. After that, I will be travelling to London myself and can escort you.'

'Charmed,' murmured Lady Godolphin, throwing him a languishing look. The effect was rather marred by one of her false eyebrows which had slipped down over her right eye.

'See here,' spluttered the vicar, 'I ain't leaving a girl of tender years *here.*'

Better here than there,' snapped Lady Godolphin. 'Pembury ain't a saint, but he don't throw his leg over the servant girls.'

'Who says I bedded Sarah?' demanded the vicar.

'I should think everyone between Hopeworth and Hopeminster by now,' flashed Lady Godolphin.

The vicar began hotly to protest his innocence. Frederica stood, dazed and bewildered. She would rather have gone to London with Lord Sylvester and stayed with Minerva. But Minerva needed rest. And Freddie, for all her timid nature, was no longer afraid of Lady Godolphin. It was very hard to be afraid of a lady who was championing one so

62

fiercely. Also, she did not know what to make of the duke's unexpected generosity. She only knew that under all her jumbled thoughts, she felt a warm glow.

The duke did not know what to make of his generosity himself. As Lady Godolphin and Mr Armitage battled away, he glanced at the small, shrinking figure of Frederica and wondered what had possessed him to offer his home and his escort to a schoolgirl and to that outrageous Malaprop.

Frederica felt very much a child, standing looking on while the grown-ups battled savagely over affairs that were still beyond her innocent comprehension. But she did not want Sarah as a stepmother.

'I must ask you to restrain yourselves,' said the duke at last, his cold voice cutting across the squabble.

The vicar and Lady Godolphin fell silent.

'I would like matters to be settled in some way,' said Lord Sylvester. 'I have already been away from my wife for too long. Frederica. What do you think? Do you wish to remain here?'

Frederica looked at the duke. But he was not looking at her. He was standing with his arm along the marble mantel, gazing into the fire. If she returned with Lord Sylvester, surely she could be of help in taking care of Minerva. On the other hand, Lord Sylvester and Minerva were so very much in love that any third person seemed like an intruder. The duke looked up at Frederica, and smiled, his eyes holding her own for a brief moment.

'Yes,' said Frederica breathlessly. 'Yes, I will stay with Lady Godolphin.'

'I think you may safely leave matters to me,' said

the Duke of Pembury. 'Miss Armitage will come to no harm in my care.'

Black eyes met green in a steady stare as the duke and Lord Sylvester took each other's measure. Then Lord Sylvester suddenly smiled. 'Yes,' he said. 'I *do* think it safe to leave Frederica with you.'

*　　　*　　　*

Lady Caroline James was in a very bad temper indeed. Without precisely asking her to leave, the duke had pointedly remarked that her invitation had been a mistake and that he was sure she would not have accepted had she known.

Nonetheless, she had great hopes of reanimating the duke's affections, but Lady Godolphin had made her continued stay impossible with her loud, vulgar remarks.

Then there was that wispy Frederica-thing. Lady James hated Frederica Armitage and blamed her for her own enforced leave-taking. That girl had masqueraded as a chambermaid under another name, and when she had been unmasked, instead of being packed off in disgrace, she had aroused knight-errant feelings in the Duke of Pembury that no one had hitherto suspected existed.

Had the duke not decided to try to pretend to be a saint in front of the colourless Miss Armitage then he would surely have looked once again on her own undoubted charms with affection.

But Lady James was clever enough not to stay in a place where she was being shown to increasing disadvantage. She made a graceful and affectionate leavetaking, and did it so well that the duke had smiled at her for the first time and had said very warmly that he hoped to call on her in town.

Lady James's ego had, however, been sadly bruised. Only now was she realizing how much the end of her lucrative affair with the Duke of Pembury had hurt her. While she had been his mistress, society had fawned on her and courted her. Once the affair was over, it became all too clear that she was regarded, despite her title,, as a member of the Fashionable Impure. Lady James now craved respectability almost as much as she craved money and jewels. When the invitation to Hatton Abbey had arrived, she had hoped he not only meant to renew the affair but perhaps to propose marriage as well. Before her affair with the duke, Lady James had always been the one to terminate the affair, enjoying the white-faced misery of her rejected lovers. She had not wanted to marry again. Now, she longed for marriage.

She took out her temper on the servants at the posting house where she had decided to break her journey on the road back to London.

She raged when she found there was no private parlour available. She stormed that she would not eat in the common dining room. While she berated the poor landlord, the noise of her tirade through the open door of her bedchamber attracted the attention of a tall gentleman who was making his way along the passage.

He stepped into the room. 'May I be of service, ma'am?' he asked. 'I have a private parlour. You are welcome to it, or, better still, I would esteem it a great honour if you would be my guest for dinner.'

Lady James smiled, a wide cat-like smile. The man was handsome and well-dressed, and she badly needed proof that her charms were still as potent as ever.

'I should be delighted . . . Mr . . ?'

'Wentwater,' said the man. 'Guy Wentwater, at your service.'

*   *   *

Perhaps the vicar of St Charles and St Jude, the Reverend Charles Armitage, felt his fall from respectability as keenly as Lady James.

Frederica had given him a rather scared little 'goodbye' and had made it quite obvious she preferred to stay in a houseful of strangers rather than return to Hopeworth with her father.

When Mrs Armitage had been alive, the vicar's affairs had been brief and discreet. But Sarah's lusty youth and blooming looks had made him throw discretion to the winds.

Since he had travelled to Hatton Abbey in Lord Sylvester's carriage, John Summer had had to drive over in the vicarage carriage to bring the reverend home.

The vicar heard the tale of Sarah's unfaithfulness with a mixture of relief and anger. He was relieved that he now had a perfect excuse for getting rid of Sarah. He was furious that that old thorn in the flesh of the Armitages, Guy Wentwater, had had the nerve to come back.

Guy Wentwater had been courting Annabelle, but when the Armitages found he was a slave trader, they had forbidden him to call, and the vicar had subsequently hounded him out of the country. He had returned to try his luck with Deirdre, but had failed. Deirdre had made a fool of him. He had then gone to America after shooting his partner

66

in crime, Silas Dubois, through the head. Since Dubois had been about to be accused of attempted murder, it was understood that Wentwater had shot him in self-defence, and so Wentwater had left for America a hero. The vicar now heard with grim satisfaction the end of Wentwater's hopes of marriage to Emily. Sir Edwin had for a long time turned a deaf ear to his brother's complaints about Guy Wentwater. He would need to pay heed now.

As they approached Hopeworth, the vicar was reluctant to go straight to the vicarage where Sarah had been locked in her old room by Mrs Hammer. His conscience, in the shape of Squire Radford, loomed up in his mind's eye. Better get that confrontation over with. Besides, he would need the squire's help.

John Summer took the carriage on to the vicarage and Ram, the squire's Indian servant, let the vicar into the hall of the squire's pleasant cottage *ornée*. The squire was in the library, sitting in a high-backed chair wearing an old-fashioned chintz coat and knee breeches.

'Sit down, Charles,' he said in a mild voice. 'We have much to discuss.'

Looking rather like a sulky child, the vicar sat down.

'I'm more sinned against than sinning,' began the vicar.

'I was prepared to marry that girl, and she ups and cuckolds me with Wentwater. Why did ye not warn me that Wentwater was back? I thought Edwin might have had the decency to tell me as well.'

'I gather he only arrived a few days ago and has only just left. I have, as you know, been kept

67

indoors with rheumatism and so I am behind hand with the gossip.

'But on the other hand,' said Squire Radford, pouring his friend a glass of wine, 'the idea of marriage to you must have turned a girl like Sarah's head. She was threatening to dismiss all your domestics once you were married. She has made no secret of the fact that you had carnal knowledge of her, Charles.'

'She zaggerates,' said the vicar. 'Why ain't she with child then? Answer me that.'

'Green elm, Charles. An old country remedy.'

'Never heard o' it. Do they dance round it at midnight, or what?'

'No. They insert a small plug of it and the green elm swells up inside to form an effective stopper.'

'Ah, yes,' said the vicar wisely, but truth to tell he had no knowledge of how this simple country method of birth control worked. He had only a vague idea of what caused the birth of a child as far as the inner workings of a woman's body were concerned. One put it in, had some energetic exercise, and if a baby resulted, then it all went to show one was not sterile or barren.

But he did grasp that Sarah had taken steps to ensure she did not get pregnant. 'Must be a tart,' he growled. 'Stands to reason.'

'I was merely speculating about the reason for her lack of pregnancy. The point is what are you going to do about the girl now, Charles?'

The vicar looked amazed. 'Do with her? Turn her out o' doors, of course.'

'On the contrary, you may be forced to marry her.'

'And just who is going to force me?'

'Your conscience, Charles. Had you treated the silly girl like a servant, then she would not have entertained ideas above her station. Nor would she, I am persuaded, have leapt so easily into bed with Wentwater. If you do not marry her yourself, then a marriage must be arranged for her.'

'Get someone to take my leavings,' said the vicar.

'Really, Charles! Do you not have one spark of feeling for the girl at all?'

The vicar sighed heavily. The clock ticked and the rain which had started to fall beat against the windows. The truth was he now wished he had never set eyes on Sarah. And yet he could not believe his luck the night she had walked into his bedroom, claiming she had seen a ghost. He had had a delicious time of it comforting her. The fact that one so gloriously young should seem to favour him had quite gone to his head. But men like the squire would never understand that there were girls who were quite as adept and cunning at the game of seduction as any man alive.

He thought of Sarah as some unfortunate indulgence, like getting too drunk, an excess best forgotten.

But he said, 'Of course I'm still fond of the girl. I'd best go speak to her and see what can be arranged.'

The vicar looked hopefully at the squire as he spoke. But for once the squire had no easy solution to one of the vicar's problems.

'What of Frederica?' asked the squire.

The vicar helped himself to more wine, pleased to have a respite from the topic of Sarah. He enlarged on Frederica's adventures, ending up complaining it was a sad day when his daughter

69

elected to stay with a rake rather than return home with her own father.

'Pembury,' said the squire reflectively, making a steeple of his fingers and looking over the top of them at the vicar. 'Very wild, he was. Settled down now, I hear. Rich *and* handsome. A devil with the ladies. Likes highflyers. And yet he ups and offers little Frederica house room and, not only that, he says he will escort her to London.'

A gleam of hope appeared in the vicar's little eyes. 'D'ye think . . .?'

'Not for a moment, Charles. Not for a moment. Flying *much* too high. No, I fear it pleases our grand duke to be kind to a schoolgirl. But what effect will his attentions have on someone so dreamy and romantical as Frederica? After you have done your best for Sarah, I think you should travel to town to enlist the support of your other daughters to find a young man for Frederica.'

'But only Minerva will be there for the Season.'

'Then write to the others. They will rally round.'

'Easily done,' said the vicar. Then his face fell. 'I wish the problem of Sarah would prove to be as easy.'

The vicar lingered over his wine for as long as possible, hoping the squire would offer to accompany him to the vicarage, but when the squire showed no signs of leaving his comfortable fireside, the vicar at last made a reluctant departure.

The Reverend Charles Armitage walked with head bowed through the driving rain. He had not felt quite so guilty or miserable since the death of his wife. He turned in at the lych gate and walked into the church yard. With dragging feet, he approached his wife's grave.

70

Slowly, he removed his hat. 'It wasn't my fault, Mrs Armitage,' he said. 'You know how flighty Sarah is. Why does the man always get the blame? The thing is . . . what am I to do? I wouldn't have been in this mess if you'd been alive. Frederica's gone off me something terrible. You know I was always faithful to you in my way. Never fouled my own doorstep before this. But what am I to do with the girl?'

The rain thudded down on the grave and trickled like tears down the white marble face of the angel perched on the headstone.

But Mrs Armitage had never been able to solve any of the vicar's problems when she was alive, largely because she never really listened to any of them, and, although all at once he missed her sorely, he knew all he was likely to get from standing in the pouring rain addressing her headstone was a bad case of rheumatics.

With a gusty sigh he turned away and let himself into the gloom of the church. He got down on his knees with great reluctance to pray. If His eye was on the sparrow, then He certainly knew all about the sins of one country vicar.

The vicar racked his mind for some sort of sacrifice to placate this God whom he always saw as a William Blake creation, all beard and bushy eyebrows, rather like an elderly military man, prone to gout.

He had given up hunting before, but God hadn't seemed to be particularly interested in that sacrifice. The obvious answer was to marry Sarah. He groaned aloud at the thought. He had a sudden vision of what Sarah would look like in ten years' time, fat and blowsy and shrewish.

'Not that,' he pleaded aloud. 'Oh, God, if only someone would marry the girl.'

'I will,' said a voice behind him.

The vicar gave a superstitious shiver. 'Who is there?' he whispered.

'It is I. Mr Pettifor.'

'What are you doin' sneaking up on a man at his prayers?' demanded the vicar, springing to his feet, and then letting out another groan as pains shot through his stiff, cold legs.

'You did not notice me, Mr Armitage,' said Mr Pettifor. 'It seemed an answer to *my* prayers when I heard you. I am prepared to marry Sarah Millet, if she will have me.'

The vicar turned and muttered a hasty 'thank you' in the direction of the altar. Then he turned back and beamed at his curate.

'Bless you, my boy,' he said. 'Your great sacrifice will not go unrewarded.'

Mr Pettifor pulled his long nose thoughtfully with his thumb and forefinger. He had been on the point of saying that marriage to Sarah was what he wanted more than anything in the world. He did not think her immoral. He thought she had been badly led astray by two such rake-hells as Guy Wentwater and Mr Armitage. The curate found his vicar's coarseness and free and easy morals a hard cross to bear, but had gradually come to believe that God was testing his faith by sending him to work for Mr Armitage.

Desire for Sarah had given his thoughts a decidedly worldly turn, and he was sure that a girl with a love of pretty dresses and ribbons might reject a penniless curate, no matter how desperate that girl might be.

He said slowly, 'It is indeed a great sacrifice. Let us hope Sarah will accept me.'

'She'd better.'

'I think she would be prepared for marriage to me had she a pleasant home to go to. As you know, I have a one-room lodging above the bakery. On the other hand, Mr Partridge died last month and you hold the lease of his cottage. It has a fine vegetable garden, and, provided you saw that I had enough money to support a wife and children, I think I might be able to persuade Sarah.'

The vicar scowled. He did not like parting with money unless it was put to some good use such as buying better hounds and better hunters.

'You said my great sacrifice would not go unrewarded,' prodded Mr Pettifor gently.

'I meant by Him,' said the vicar, pointing up to the roof with a sanctimonious expression on his face.

'Ah, yes,' said Mr Pettifor. 'But you, Mr Armitage, are His humble instrument. Of course, perhaps He feels you should marry Sarah yourself.'

The vicar began to look alarmed.

'Furthermore,' pursued Mr Pettifor, 'I think perhaps the sacrifice might be too great. After all, it was not I who seduced the girl.'

'Anything you want, Pettifor,' said the vicar hurriedly. 'Money, cottage, garden . . . anything.'

'Then perhaps you will come with me? Poor Sarah has been locked in her room by Mrs Hammer.'

The rain was so heavy by the time they reached the end of the short drive that led to the vicarage that they could hardly see the building itself.

They entered the hall and were met by Rose who

73

removed their coats and urged them in a hushed voice to go into the parlour where the fire was made up—'but 'tain't drawing too well.'

The vicar looked approvingly at Rose's long sheeplike face. From now on, he vowed, any female servant he engaged would be the plainest he could find.

'I think we should see Sarah first,' said Mr Pettifor, showing budding signs of authority. 'Please tell Mrs Hammer to unlock her room.'

Mrs Hammer came hurrying out of the kitchen, clutching a key in her hand, and pushing wisps of grey hair up under her cap. Her broad face looked disapproving and sullen. She led the way up the stairs.

The vicarage had been a pleasant home, reflected Mr Pettifor, when Mrs Armitage had been alive and all the girls unmarried. Now all signs of femininity were fled, despite the female servants, leaving it very much a bachelor residence, smelling of smoky fires, damp dogs and brandy.

Sarah's room was in one of the attics at the top of the house. As they climbed higher, they could hear the rain drumming and pounding on the roof as if trying to get in.

'Dreadful storm,' said the vicar. 'Better get this pesky business over and make sure hounds' kennels ain't leaking.'

Mr Pettifor primmed his lips in disapproval. Poor Sarah was probably breaking her heart while her hardhearted seducer worried about a pack of smelly dogs.

The vicar was prepared for a defiant, noisy Sarah. A great wave of guilt hit him when he saw the dejected figure sitting on the edge of the bed.

Her eyes were red with crying and her hair was unkempt.

Sarah had had quite a time on her own to consider her dismal future. Mrs Hammer had dinned into her ears tales of the iniquities of Guy Wentwater and how he would do anything to get even with the vicar. She knew she could not even expect to get a reference. She had no family and no savings. A vision of the workhouse in Hopeminster rose before her mind's eye.

As the vicar entered the room, she bowed her head, awaiting her fate.

'Well, Sarah,' said the vicar hurriedly, 'seems you've suffered enough. Mr Pettifor here wants a word with you.'

The vicar backed to the door. Mr Pettifor sidled round him.

'Miss Millet,' said Mr Pettifor. 'I would be honoured . . . deeply honoured . . . if you would present me with your hand in marriage.'

Sarah blinked, and then a hard, sullen look fell on her face. 'He forced you to ask,' she said, jerking her thumb in the direction of the vicar who was backing out onto the landing.

Mr Pettifor knelt in front of the maid and took her hand in his own.

'No one could force me to marry anyone, Miss Millet. I love you, and I think you are the most wonderful lady I ever beheld.'

The effect of his words on Sarah was amazing.

For a moment, she sat and stared at the curate. Then it seemed as if the red left her eyes like magic, that her lank hair curled up about her head, that she seemed to shine from head to foot.

'Oh, Mr *Pettifor*,' she breathed. 'Thank you, ever

so.'

The Reverend Charles Armitage felt more lighthearted than he had felt for a long time. He cheerfully slammed the door on the happy couple and went off down the stairs, whistling 'The Lass of Richmond Hill'.

He headed out the front door and made for the kennels. Now he could turn his mind to more serious matters.

CHAPTER FIVE

Frederica Armitage did not entertain any romantic ideas about the Duke of Pembury. She was too much in awe of him. In fact, she was too much in awe of everyone. She felt the unspoken disapproval of the Duke of Pembury's servants, and, as far as the house guests were concerned, she barely existed.

Dinner was an agony of trying to think what to say. Lady Godolphin was flirting awfully with an elderly county gentleman and did not concern herself overmuch with Frederica. There were no men present whom Lady Godolphin considered of a suitable age for Frederica, and, therefore, she had planned to reserve her match-making energies until she got the girl to London.

Only Mary, the maid, remained the same, cheerful and willing, and excited at the prospect of going to London.

Shy and sensitive, Frederica did not realize the unfriendliness she sensed was not directed against herself. The house party was not a success. Normally, the gentlemen would have gone out

76

hunting or shooting during the day and the ladies would have gone for picnics and walks.

But the rain fell heavily, steadily and unremittingly, so everyone was confined indoors. Since no one but Frederica and the duke read much, the guests ate too much and spent the afternoons in a somnolent state and then passed the long evenings cheating each other at cards.

As for the duke, he seemed too busy with the affairs of his vast estates to trouble himself much about his guests. By supplying vast quantities of food and drink, billiards and cards, the duke felt he was doing his duty as a host and never once thought of organizing amateur theatricals, games or charades, or anything else that might have relieved the boredom.

The duke himself did not enjoy house parties but felt it his duty to return hospitality by inviting as many people to stay at the one time, and so getting the boring business of returning entertainment over with in one go.

He was regretting his offer to escort Lady Godolphin and Miss Armitage to London. Miss Armitage had failed to hold his interest. Every time he saw her, she either had her head in a book or was sitting, dumb and embarrassed, at his dinner table.

As the rain continued to fall, the guests began to take their leave, tedium driving away even the most determined sponger.

At last, there were only Lady Godolphin and Frederica left.

The duke sent a message to Lady Godolphin suggesting they make their departure for London before the roads became any worse. The servants and luggage were to precede them in two carriages so that they would be waiting at each posting house for the duke to arrive. Frederica was disappointed. She had hoped to enjoy Mary's cheerful company on the journey.

They set out on a miserable morning with the rain pitting the lakes which had formed on the lawns in front of the house.

Frederica and Lady Godolphin were to travel with the duke in his carriage.

To Frederica's relief, Lady Godolphin talked nonstop for most of the morning as the carriage rumbled through a rain-drenched countryside. Finally, the duke, seeming to become weary of trying to understand her malapropisms, fell asleep.

'Such a handsome man,' sighed Lady Godolphin. 'Deep in the arms of Murphy, he is. I do hope he has made arrangements to break our journey soon for it is wearisome when you can't see anything but rain and more rain.'

The carriage lamps had been lit because it had grown almost as black as night. A wind had risen and was driving great sheets of water against the carriage windows. Frederica began to feel sick with the lurching and swaying of the carriage. Lady Godolphin had fallen asleep as well, her turbanned head bobbing up and down as the carriage pitched like a ship on the high seas.

Frederica took out a book but found all she could make out was the whiteness of the page. The lamps inside the carriage had not been lit and she did not have a tinder box. All she could see of the duke opposite was the paleness of his face and cravat against the black of his clothes. He seemed to wear a great deal of black.

She wondered if the duke had ever been in love or if he had always simply 'shopped' for one. The face Lady James showed the duke was a very different one from the one she showed the servants. When he was anywhere on the scene, she became all soft voice and melting glances. Frederica gave herself a shake. She did not want to think of the duke with Lady James any more than she wanted to think about her father with Sarah.

Frederica fumbled in her reticule for her vinaigrette. She wished she had the courage to wake the duke and beg him to stop the carriage.

'We have been travelling for *hours*,' thought Frederica dismally. 'He surely does not mean to drive until nightfall. Oh, if only this sickening motion would *stop!*'

Unconsciously, she had said the last words aloud. The duke's eyes opened. 'What is the matter?' he asked.

'I f-feel s-sick,' stammered Frederica. '*I am* going to be sick.'

The duke picked up his silver-headed swordstick and pushed up the trap in the roof, letting in a small flood of water right on Lady Godolphin's head.

'Follicles!' spluttered that lady. 'What's to do?'

'Miss Armitage is sick,' said the duke calmly He called to his coachman, 'Bob, hold the horses.' There was a hoarse reply and to Frederica it seemed as if the whole shaking, swaying world had miraculously righted itself. But her stomach still heaved.

'I had better get down,' she said.

'Nonsense,' said the Duke of Pembury. 'Stick your head out of the window.'

'*I can't*,' protested Frederica miserably. 'It is too

undignified.'

'God grant me strength. Very well. Get down.' He jerked the strap and opened the carriage door. A groom jumped from the backstrap and let down the steps.

'This man will catch his death of cold!' exclaimed Frederica, looking at the sodden groom.

The duke gritted his teeth. 'Are you going to stand there all day, Miss Armitage? Or are you doing to get down?'

Drawing a carriage rug tightly about her shoulders, for she was only wearing a thin muslin gown and a pelisse made out of one of Lady Godolphin's gowns by that lady's excellent maid, Frederica launched out into the storm.

If she went around the front of the coach, then she would make an exhibition of herself in front of the coachman. At either side, she might be seen by the duke or Lady Godolphin; at the back, by the grooms.

She headed for the side of the road and began to walk through a small wood until she was sure she was well out of sight of the carriage, although a few steps would have been enough to take her out of sight of any onlooker since the day was so black and the storm so wild.

It was then she realized to her chagrin that she was not feeling in the slightest bit sick, although she was now soaked and shivering. Feeling very silly, she started to make her way towards the carriage.

But where was the carriage?

There was only the sound of the wind tearing through the trees above and the pounding of the rain. She could not see the carriage lights, nor could she hear any voices. She did not want

80

to cause further trouble by calling out for help, thereby forcing one of those poor servants to come and look for her. It certainly changed one's view of life, having been a servant oneself, even for such a short time.

'I must not panic,' thought Frederica. 'I am not the same as I was. I am Courageous and Resolute. The carriage is surely over there.'

Putting her head down, she ran off into the roaring blackness. She could vaguely make out that the trees were thinning. She must be near the road.

And then, all of a sudden, her foot slipped and she plunged down and down, finally clashing into a bush. Winded and terrified, Frederica lay still. She was sure she had broken every bone in her body. After a few moments, she cautiously moved her arms and legs. She was frightened to get to her feet in case she might fall again.

'Help!' she called as loudly as she could, although the wind seemed to snatch up her voice and tear it to shreds.

She peered upwards, narrowing her eyes against the rain, hoping to see the bobbing light of a lantern, for surely they must be searching for her by now. But the whole world had turned into a roaring blackness of rain and wind and there was no light in sight.

Frederica cautiously got to her feet, wincing with pain as her wet clothes clung to her bruised and scraped legs and arms, She tried to struggle up the slope, missed her footing, and started to slither downwards, grabbing frantically at grass and roots to try to slow the increasing speed of her descent.

At last she stopped as her feet struck against rock. Frederica no longer thought of trying to make her way back to the carriage. Her one thought was to find some sort of shelter, and try to stay alive.

She twisted about and looked down. Through the dimness, she could make out a stream, tumbling along just below her feet. Frederica took a deep breath. The stream must lead somewhere, and somewhere might lead back to the road,

Slowly and painfully, she began to pick her way along the tumbled rocks and grass beside the edge of the river. She began to talk aloud to keep her spirits up. 'It is a miracle,' said Frederica stoutly, 'that I have not even twisted an ankle. I am very cold and wet and hungry, but I am sure I will find somewhere soon. I must have lost the carriage rug in my fall, but that is of no matter. It would have been too heavy and cumbersome.'

The rain gradually grew less and the sky grew lighter although the wind seemed to have increased in force. Frederica could now make out a thin path beside the river which twisted round the rocks and boulders and hummocks of grass. Now that she could see it, the going was easier.

The sky grew lighter still.

She looked up and saw with a kind of awe that the river was at the bottom of a gorge and realised she was very lucky indeed not to have broken her neck.

It was too steep on either side of the river to think of trying to climb up, so all she could do was plod along the path. She hoped the little track had been made by humans rather than animals like rabbits.

She was very tired, very cold, and very hungry. Why had no one come in search of her? Had the autocratic duke simply told his servants to drive on?

But Lady Godolphin would never allow that. Frederica thought rather tearfully of Lady Godolphin's championship.

At last, she sat down on a rock and stared miserably at the rushing stream. The rain had stopped and the sky was clearing to the west. But it was growing darker again.

'I must have been walking for hours,' thought Frederica. 'Night must be falling, and, oh, it is so cold. I *must* not sit here. My clothes are too thin. Get yourself up and keep walking.'

But when she rose to her feet, her legs trembled with fatigue and her teeth chattered with cold. Now, her progress was slow as her increasingly dragging steps followed the ever-rushing river.

Then, in the increasing gloom, Frederica saw the shape of what looked like a building.

Shelter!

She ran towards it, frightened it might turn out to be a square-shaped mass of rock.

But it was a building . . . of sorts. It was a stone square with two small boarded-up windows and a wooden door.

'It must be a water bailiff's hut,' thought Frederica, disappointed that there were no signs of life. She tried the door. It was firmly locked.

That was when Frederica sat down and began to cry in earnest. For one blissful moment, she had thought her nightmare was over.

The wind whipped her wet clothes against her body. 'Are you going to sit here and *die* of exposure, you silly widgeon?' Frederica admonished herself. Break the door down.'

'I can't,' wailed the old timid Frederica. 'I haven't the strength.'

'Of course you have,' chided the new Frederica. 'Pick up a rock and break the lock. Go *on!*'

Still sobbing, Frederica got up and picked up as heavy a rock as she could manage to handle. Holding it in both hands, she swung it sideways against the lock with as much force as she could muster. There was a satisfactory splitting of wood and the door slowly creaked open. Frederica felt her way into the black interior. She opened the shutters on one small window. There was no glass and the wind came whistling in. But the sky had cleared and a small moon was rising. From its weak light, Frederica was able to make out some objects in the room. There was a table and one chair. Some fishing rods were propped against the wall. On the table was the white stick of a tallow candle.

Frederica groped her way over to the table and felt across its surface with her fingers. They closed with triumph on a tinder box and an oily piece of cotton waste. She lit the cotton and then the candle, quickly shielding the flame from the wind blowing in the window. Then she set the candle on the floor, out of the draught, and closed the shutters.

She picked the candle up again and set it on the table. There was a small black iron stove against the far wall and, on a shelf above it, two more candles stuck in bottles. Frederica lit both of them and turned her attention to the stove. There were a few sticks of kindling beside it and an old newspaper, but no logs. Perhaps there might be some outside, stacked at the side or the back of the hut.

The wind moaned around the building. Gritting her teeth, Frederica went outside again. Black clouds were rushing across the moon, plunging everything into Stygian darkness.

'I hope I never go blind,' muttered Frederica, stumbling over something at the corner of the but and badly grazing her knee. At the back of the hut, she felt some rough sacking and fumbled under it.

Logs! And plenty of them.

She filled her arms with them and made her way carefully back round to the front, shouldering her way in the door, and kicking it shut behind her with one foot before the candles could blow out.

She pulled open the iron top of the stove and filled it with paper, kindling and logs, and then lit it with one of the candles. With a satisfactory roar, the fire began to burn.

She pulled the chair up to the stove, opened the little door at the front, and spread her fingers out before the blaze.

'I've done it!' thought Frederica with a sort of wonder. 'I am alive. I have survived . . .'

She looked about her. The hut consisted of this one small room. Beside the fishing rods were some old game bags. There was no bed. It was obviously used by the water bailiff to rest during his patrols up and down the river, and probably also by gamekeepers. There was a tiny wooden dresser with pewter mugs in one corner. Frederica went over and looked in the cupboard underneath. There was half a loaf of stale bread, and beside the dresser, on the floor, a small cask of cider.

Frederica found a knife in the dresser drawer and tried to cut the bread. It was very hard but she managed to hack off a chunk. Then she poured herself a mug of cider and returned to the fire. The stale bread dipped in the cider tasted marvellous. Her eyes began to droop as the heat from the fire made her clothes steam. She removed her bonnet and looked sadly at the wreck of it. Searching in her sodden reticule which had miraculously remained attached to her wrist through all her adventures, she found her comb and began to comb out her wet hair in front of the fire.

But after a time, even the effort of combing seemed too much for her tired arms.

She collected the game bags and made a lumpy sort of mattress of them in front of the fire on the earth floor. It was wonderful to lie down and stretch out in warmth and safety. The buckles of the canvas game bags were digging into her but she hardly noticed.

Her eyes began to close.

She awoke an hour later. The wind had died down and so had the fire. She had blown out the candles and so the room was lit only by the faint red glow of the stove. She stumbled to her feet, groaning with all her aches and pains, and threw more logs on the fire, waiting until it was cheerfully blazing again, before settling down to sleep once more.

And then she heard a loud curse.

Frederica sat up. She must be imagining things. Although the wind had dropped, the rushing of the stream filled the air.

She was just about to lie down again when she distinctly heard footsteps.

She rose to her feet and faced the door. If it was the water bailiff then she would have a lot of explaining to do. But what if it was a footpad?

Slowly, the door creaked open and a tall figure loomed on the threshold.

Frederica gave a faint scream.

'If, as I believe, you prove to be Miss Armitage,'

said a deep, masculine voice, 'then it is going to give me great pleasure to wring your neck.'

'It is you,' said Frederica weakly. 'It is Pembury.'

The Duke of Pembury strode into the room, kicking the door shut behind him. He lit one of the candles and held it up and surveyed Frederica. He had been about to shout at her, to curse her for her folly, to damn her for frightening him out of his wits, but when he saw the slight figure in the torn and muddy dress and noticed the scratches and bruises on her face, he said instead, 'You gave me the deuce of a fright.'

'Is Lady Godolphin with you?' asked Frederica.

'No, of course she is not with me,' he said testily. 'The path you took is enough to kill anything other than a mountain goat. When you did not return, I and my servants searched and searched for you. A farmer came by in a gig and told us there was an inn just around the next bend. We felt sure you must have found your way there. But when we got to the inn we found you were still lost. Lady Godolphin was wailing to heaven that you had surely been taken by footpads and were now being "ravishinged".

'We spread out in different directions. I eventually found the route you had taken by falling over the cliff in the dark and losing my lantern. I ended up against a bush and found a scrap of torn muslin on one of the branches. The moon was coming out and so I managed to follow your tracks. It was just beginning to rain again before I reached here. I had lost all trace of you since the ground had become hard and rocky and I began to fear you had fallen in the stream.

'But here you are, complete with roof over your

head and fire on the hearth. I don't know whether to beat you or burst into tears with sheer relief.'

'I am so sorry,' said Frederica. 'Please do not be angry.'

'We can't stay here,' he said wearily. 'You will be compromised.'

'Is it very far to this inn?'

'Miles and miles. You walked quite a distance, my sweeting.'

The wind howled, and the rain, once more increasing in force, beat against the shutters.

Frederica shivered. 'Upon my life,' she said, 'I would as lief be ruined as dead.'

The duke swung his heavy cloak from his shoulders and took off his hat. 'We will wait for a little, Miss Armitage. But if the storm does not abate, then journey on we must.'

He spread his coat over the game bags on the floor in front of the fire. 'Fortunately my clothes did not receive a wetting. Sit here by me on my cloak, Miss Armitage.'

Frederica looked at him nervously. His face looked satanic in the leaping flames of the stove.

He sat down and looked up at her. 'Do not be missish. I have no intention of seducing you.'

She sat down next to him, bolt upright, staring at the flames as if she had never seen anything so interesting in all her life.

'Relax.' He put an arm about her shoulders and drew her to him. 'Now, sleep. I will stay awake and I will rouse you in about half an hour.'

Frederica lay rigid in the circle of his arm. 'What an unusual situation,' she thought. He neither moved nor said anything and at last her eyelids began to droop. Her body relaxed against him.

With a weary little sigh, she laid her head on his chest and fell fast asleep.

He smoothed back her hair which was tickling his chin. It was very fine hair, like a baby's. What a frail little thing she seemed, and yet she had proved remarkably adept at looking after herself. He began to feel very tired. Still holding Frederica, he wrenched off his cravat and threw it across the room. His coat felt tight and uncomfortable. He laid the still sleeping Frederica down on his cloak and divested himself of his coat, waistcoat and boots. It would do no harm to have half an hour's sleep himself.

The duke lay down beside Frederica in front of the fire and gathered her into his arms. She murmured something in her sleep but did not awake.

Frederica was having a deliciously shocking dream. She was swimming in a warm blue sea without one stitch of clothing on. The water caressed her limbs and little silver fish darted to and fro among large pink rocks which stood up from the ocean floor. And then a merman started to swim towards her. She was not afraid of him, and when he took her in his arms, it seemed the most natural thing in the world to kiss him.

Just as Frederica was kissing the merman in her dreams, the duke woke up, half wondering where he was. The girl was pressed tightly against his chest and he could feel her small breasts through the thin cambric of his shirt. Her body was causing a tingling feeling of excitement to run through his own.

He sleepily put his hand under her chin and bent his mouth to hers. Frederica, in her dream, was passionately returning the merman's kisses. The

Duke of Pembury found himself at the receiving end of one of Frederica's most passionate offerings. He thought he had never felt such a burning sweetness from a kiss in all his life. His lips buried deeper and his expert hands lazily caressed the slim young body pressed so tightly against his own.

And then a voice seemed to scream in his head. 'It's that Armitage girl, you fool!' He rolled away and jerked himself upright and started piling logs onto the fire.

He twisted around. Frederica was, miraculously, still asleep, but a long sunbeam was shining through a chink in the wooden shutters.

'Hell and damnation,' said the Duke of Pembury bitterly. 'Compromised. And by a schoolgirl. What the deuce kept me asleep so long?'

Frederica's eyes flew open at the sound of his voice and she stared up at him. Her eyes were great dark pools in the dim light of the hut.

'Aye, you may stare, miss,' snapped the duke. 'I over-slept and thanks to your folly in losing yourself, I will now have to marry you. You!'

Frederica sat up, her face flaming.

'If you think for one minute, your grace, that I am going to tell *anyone* that I spent the night alone with you in this hut, you are very much mistaken.'

'Do you mean to say, you *don't* want to marry me?' The Duke of Pembury looked at Frederica with an expression of shock mixed with disbelief in his black eyes.

'Of course not, your grace,' said Frederica. She laughed. 'You are *much* too old.'

He should have felt relief, he knew that. On the other hand his whole mind was screaming out that he had never been so insulted in all his life.

Since he came of age, he had been fighting off debutantes. He knew that any girl or woman at the Season would rush into his arms at the slightest invitation.

He shrugged himself into his coat. 'I am possibly too mature for you for you are sadly childish. I will appreciate your discretion. You may cover yourself with my cloak. If asked where I found you, I will say I found you as you were leaving here this morning. Come along.'

He strode to the door and wrenched it open. 'I hope all men are not so bad-tempered,' thought Frederica dismally. 'For my family is sure to find me a husband and they will nag me to death if I do not marry.'

She bundled the folds of the duke's cloak about her and followed him out of the hut.

The air was fresh and sweet. Birds were chirping in the bushes and a mellow sun shone over the rain-sodden steeps of the gorge.

The duke was striding up the path without looking behind him.

'I cannot run after him,' thought Frederica, 'and leave the fire still burning and the game bags on the floor.'

She hurried back into the hut and began to clear up. The duke made his reappearance just as she was pouring a pewter mug of cider over the fire.

'Do you plan to stay here all day?' he demanded.

'I was merely putting things in order,' said Frederica mildly. 'Your cravat is still lying in the corner where you seem to have dropped it.'

The duke picked it up and stuffed it in his pocket. He realized she had the right of it. It was folly to march off, leaving the hut with all the evidence that two people had passed the night there.

When they were finally on their road, he saw, in the full sunlight, that her clothes were torn and muddy and that she was stumbling wearily.

'Take my arm,' he said abruptly. 'We will follow the path in the opposite direction from where we came. With luck, we may soon find a road to the top.'

Frederica looked about her in a dazed way. The roaring black nightmare of the night before had been transformed into a pleasant pastoral scene. Even the river was tamer now, broader and lazier.

The path made a sudden twist away from the river and began to ascend in winding loops up the steep side of the gorge to their right.

Frederica stumbled wearily and would have fallen had he not caught her firmly round the waist. Ignoring her protests, he swung her up into his arms and set off up the path.

He walked very quickly, disturbed by the feel of her body against his chest, remembering that kiss.

Frederica was remembering her strange dream. It had seemed so real. She tried to recall the merman's face but it looked like the duke's.

There was a shout from above. The duke stopped and lowered Frederica gently to her feet. A group of militia led by their captain were hurrying down the path.

'Rescue at last,' said the duke. 'Remember. I only met you this morning.'

Frederica looked up into his eyes with a steady gaze. Then those odd eyes of hers began to sparkle with humour and that bewitching smile lit up her face. 'My dear duke,' she said gently, 'you really must believe me. I have absolutely no intention of marrying you. You must have been *very* lucky in love because you seem to find it impossible to believe I do not want you. And yet, it is almost as if you are hoping that I *will* try to compromise you in order to either justify your low opinion of my sex or to restore your bruised *amour propre.'*

'You little minx!' said the Duke of Pembury with a reluctant smile. 'I shall keep well away from you in London, or goodness knows what trouble you will embroil me in.'

*　　*　　*

At that moment, Lady James was taking a fond farewell of Mr Guy Wentwater on the steps of her London house. He had enlivened the journey for her considerably.

'I am sorry,' said Mr Wentwater, 'that you will not help me in my plans to confound the Armitages —particularly after you told me that Miss Frederica had been instrumental in speeding your departure.'

Lady James laughed. 'If I thought that tiresome little girl had attracted Pembury in the slightest, I would certainly help you in your schemes. But she was a passing whim, nothing more.'

CHAPTER SIX

It was the eve of the beginning of the London Season and Frederica's five elder sisters were gathered in Minerva's elegant drawing room for a council of war over the teacups.

Minerva was still looking pale and tired. Her children had been confined to the nursery. Deirdre had a one-year-old son and Daphne a six-month-old baby girl. It was too early yet to tell whether Diana was with child or not. But the three mothers tactfully avoided discussing babies or the possibility of babies. For Annabelle had still shown no signs of becoming pregnant and became cross and sad when her more fortunate sisters discussed their offspring.

'To business,' said Minerva, tapping her spoon against her cup. 'We are all agreed that a husband must be found for Frederica. She is a gentle, good little thing but it will take all our efforts to bring her to the notice of a suitable gentleman.'

'I think Frederica has great charm,' said Diana defiantly, her black eyes flashing. 'Why rush her into marriage? Our husbands have all contributed to give her a large dowry. She may pick and choose.'

'Frederica has a fine spirit,' said Minerva. 'But she is not precisely . . .'

'Pretty,' said Annabelle, complacently patting her golden curls.

There were cries of protest from the other four. 'Be sensible,' said Annabelle. 'We are all here to help her find a husband, because, if we do not, she may end up in the arms of a fortune hunter.'

'Is there no hope of Pembury forming a *tendre* for Frederica?' asked red-haired Deirdre. 'After all, he did rescue her.'

'I do not think any of us would wish to see our beloved Frederica married to a man such as Pentbury,' said Minerva primly. 'He has an unsavoury reputation and . . .'

'And it does not say much for darling Frederica's

94

charms that she experienced no trouble from that quarter,' said Annabelle.

'You always were a cat,' said Deirdre. 'I suppose *you* feel you would have had to fight him off. Well, let me tell you it is well known that Pembury has reformed and I had it from the Duchess of Dunster that he is looking for a wife.'

'How dare you call me a cat, carrot-top,' flashed Annabelle.

'Girls,' admonished Minerva. 'I would like to make one thing plain. This is my home and I will not have it turned into a bear garden. Control your selves. Sensible suggestions only, or remain quiet.'

'There is a certain Mr Harrison,' said Daphne. 'He has a pretty house in Sussex and a prosperous estate. He is a friend of Dantrey's. He would escort Frederica to the opera if I asked him.'

'You know,' said Deirdre reflectively, 'I called on Frederica the other day. When I asked about Pembury, she did not talk much about him but she blushed a great deal. There may be no hope of Pembury forming a *tendre* for Frederica, but I am very much afraid she has formed a *tendre* for *him*.'

'Oh, dear,' said Minerva. 'That will never do. Comfrey is anxious to take me off to the country and I am anxious . . .' She was about to say 'anxious to give the children some fresh air' but because of Annabelle, she ended, 'to have some fresh air. Now, which one of you is going to be in town?'

Annabelle frowned. 'Brabington has promised to take me to Paris.'

'Dantrey will not be coming to town,' said Diana, 'and I do not want to be separated from him. What about you, Daphne?'

But the elegant Daphne was no longer interested

in the pleasures of London. All she wanted to do was return to the country to her husband, Simon Garfield, and to her beloved baby.

'Harry and I will be in town,' said Deirdre cheerfully. Deirdre flouted convention by always referring to her husband by his first name. 'All the rest of you need to do is to send the beaux in my direction and I will take them round to Frederica.'

'In that case,' said Minerva with relief, 'we will do all we can to help you. Is there any hope you could persuade Lady Godolphin to let Frederica be brought out by you?'

'I tried,' Deirdre laughed. 'But you know how she is. She is firmly convinced that we are all married thanks to her good offices. Lady Godolphin also has Papa's blessing. But do not worry. I shall be calling on Frederica almost every day so it will almost be the same as bringing her out. Then there is the matter of her clothes. We have all sent her very pretty gowns, but somehow they do not look right on her. She needs a dressmaker with a practised eye. And *something* must be done about her hair.'

'It is very pretty when it is curled,' said Minerva, 'but after only half an hour it is again falling about her face in wisps. We will send Monsieur Andre to her and see what magic he can perform. In two days' time, she will attend the opening, ball at Almack's. She *must* look her best.'

'Don't fuss, Merva,' said Deirdre crossly. 'I am perfectly capable of taking care of Freddie.'

'Don't call her Freddie,' said Daphne. 'You make her sound like a boy. If some malicious gossip hears you, they will have the whole of the *ton* talking about "poor Freddie Armitage".'

'I do not think we should go off at tangents, discussing what we should call her,' said Diana. 'What is worrying me is Frederica's romantical disposition. Have you *seen* Pembury? He is very tall and well-built and looks like a fallen angel. If Freddie is not in love with him already I will be very much surprised. Make sure, Deirdre, that she is not allowed to be alone for a moment in his company. Tell Lady Godolphin to be on her guard. Pembury will no doubt call on her just to be polite and Frederica quite probably will read more into his call than actually exists.'

'I am a married lady now,' said Deirdre hotly. 'I am furthermore older than you, Diana, so there is no need to give me *orders*.'

'I was simply talking common-sense . . .'

'What about Papa?' demanded Minerva, cutting across Diana's angry voice.

There was a silence. Then Daphne asked, 'Why? Have you heard any bad news?'

'It is what I have *not* heard that puzzles me,' said Minerva. 'Comfrey went down to Hopeworth ostensibly to talk to Papa about a new system of land drainage. He was gone for several days. He had promised to call at the seminary and to bring Frederica back with him.

'But on his return, he said—rather vaguely— that he had learned Lady Godolphin was a house guest of Pembury, and since Hatton Abbey was quite near the seminary, he and Papa had taken Frederica there. But I had a *very* odd letter from Papa just the other day in which he bemoans the fact that Frederica preferred the company of a rake to that of her own father. But since she had never met Pembury before, how could she? Comfrey simply laughed and said that Papa had probably subsequently heard all the old scandals about Pembury and was suffering from one of his usual fits of guilt. Papa also wrote to say that everything about Sarah was "all right and tight". Comfrey said that one of the servants who must have been Sarah had had a bad fever on his visit and that Papa must have assumed I knew about it. Comfrey has never lied to me before. I think perhaps he has been keeping bad news from me because of my illness.'

'I shall call at the vicarage on my return to the country, Merva,' said Diana, 'and I will write to you as soon as possible and let you know how Papa goes on.'

'Thank you, Diana,' said Minerva. 'Now, as to suitable beaux for Frederica . . .'

The sisters put their elegant heads together and the next half-hour was pleasantly spent writing down names and discussing yearly incomes.

At last the discussion about Frederica was over. In a flurry of silks and satins, Annabelle, Deirdre, Daphne and Diana said farewell to Minerva and went out to their respective carriages.

Annabelle drew Deirdre aside on the pavement outside. 'I *am* a cat,' she said ruefully, 'but sometimes Freddie seems so vague and dreamy and *defenceless,* I could shake her.'

'I'll take care of her,' said Deirdre. 'Perhaps we should all be worrying about *you*, Annabelle. You do not seem happy. Tell me about it. I will help if I can.'

'No one can help me,' said Annabelle. 'Oh, leave me *alone*, Deirdre.'

She marched off to her carriage.

'It's that baby she longs for and cannot have,'

thought Deirdre sadly. 'If only . . .'

But she had prayed for Annabelle so many times and nothing ever seemed to happen.

With a little sigh, Deirdre mounted into her carriage. She would call on Lady Godolphin and make sure everything possible might be done to make Frederica look her best at Almack's.

*   *   *

Frederica's thoughts were, in fact, lightly turning to thoughts of love. But despite her sisters' fears, she had no particular gentleman in mind. It was as if her dream of the merman had awakened something in her. She was frightened of her debut at Almack's and began to console herself with dreams of a faceless young man who might . . . well . . . *befriend* her. They would chat together and be comfortable together and perhaps, just perhaps, at the end of the Season, he would propose. It was not as if she could hope for a dazzling marriage like any of her sisters'. Perhaps there might be a homely but pleasant young man, as shy as herself, who might take a liking to her.

Deirdre had descended on the house like a whirlwind, demanding to see her ball gown, ordering the services of Monsieur Andre to do her hair, and reducing poor Mary to tears by pointing out her deficiencies as a lady's maid.

Frederica had rushed hotly to Mary's defence, saying she had been a servant herself, and people had no idea how badly servants were treated.

Deirdre had demanded an explanation and Frederica had found herself telling Deirdre the whole story about her flight from the seminary, her job as a chambermaid, and her night in the storm. The only thing she did not tell Deirdre was that she had slept in the arms of the Duke of Pembury.

Listening with increasing horror, Deirdre finally gasped, 'Papa to marry Sarah?'

'Oh, not any more,' said Frederica. 'He wrote to Lady Godolphin. Lady Godolphin told me that Sarah had been found *in fragrant delicious* with Guy Wentwater.'

'No!'

'Oh, yes, and Sarah is to marry Mr Pettifor who, it seems, loves her very much.'

Deirdre had been so shocked by these revelations that she had quite forgotten to caution her young sister about entertaining any warm feelings towards the Duke of Pembury.

It was only when Frederica was finally being made ready for the ball at Almack's that Deirdre remembered about the duke but felt the time was not right. The duke would be at Almack's but dukes did not dance with such as Frederica Armitage. There would be time and enough to caution Frederica in the days to come.

Deirdre sat downstairs in the Yellow Saloon while Mary, Martha, Lady Godolphin's lady's maid, and Monsieur Andre slaved over Frederica's appearance.

Colonel Arthur Brian, the elderly gentleman Lady Godolphin referred to as her 'sissybo', arrived to escort that lady to the ball.

Lady Godolphin waddled in, attired in transparent pink muslin, the seductive effect of which was spoiled by the enormous blue corset she was wearing underneath and which could be plainly seen.

Deirdre had a sudden stab of panic. If Lady Godolphin's Martha allowed her mistress to go out looking like *that,* then what on earth was she doing to poor Frederica?

Lady Godolphin had angrily begun to demand of Colonel Brian where that gentleman had been during the past few weeks.

She then hurled in his face the gossip that Lady James had thrown at *her,* and it was while the colonel was hotly protesting his innocence that the door opened and Mice, Lady Godolphin's butler, ushered Frederica in.

'Oh, *no!*' moaned Deirdre. 'What have they done to you?'

Frederica was wearing a white muslin gown with a high waist. It was cut low enough to bare the inadequacies of her bosom. It had white lace sleeves and a white lace demi-train. The white seemed to draw what little colour there was about Frederica right away, leaving her looking waif-like and forlorn, like a child-bride abandoned on the steps of the church by the bridegroom who had never arrived.

Her hair was curled all over her head, stiff, metallic-looking curls embellished with white silk roses.

'Is anything the matter, Deirdre?' asked Frederica timidly. 'Mary says I do not look like myself at all, and I must confess my head hurts.'

'Then take that dreadful wig off,' snapped Deirdre.

'It isn't a wig,' said Frederica. 'My hair would not stay in its curls and so Monsieur Andre used a mixture of sugar and water to gum it together.'

'Oh, do please be quiet,' snapped Deirdre,

speaking to Lady Godolphin and Colonel Brian who were quarrelling noisily.

She called Mary forward. 'It seems you have more sense than my lady's maid and Monsieur Andre. Take Miss Armitage upstairs immediately and wash all that stuff out of her hair. I am going home to fetch a few things. She must have *colour*.'

Frederica looked to Lady Godolphin for help. It had taken *hours* of preparation: hours of being clipped and curled and dressed and perfumed. Surely, she would not have to go through it all again.

But Lady Godolphin and Colonel Brian were still scrapping. 'My love,' pleaded the colonel, 'what I need is your love.'

'What you need, my good man,' howled Lady Godolphin, 'is a kick up the testimonials.'

Deirdre gave Lady Godolphin a scandalized look and pushed Frederica out of the room. 'Quickly,' she said. 'I will not be gone long.'

By the time Frederica was finally declared ready to go to the ball, Deirdre and Mary were exhausted but triumphant.

'I think Frederica did very well to choose you as lady's maid,' said Deirdre. 'You have a good eye for colour and, what is more important, *common-sense*.'

Mary's squashed face turned beet-red with pleasure. She curtsied and murmured that she thought Miss Frederica looked 'more herself.'

Frederica was now wearing one of Deirdre's gowns. It had only needed to be taken in at the bosom to become a perfect fit. It was of pale green, very fine silk, a simple cut with a high waist and little puff sleeves. Her hair, which had a slight

102

natural curl, had been washed and brushed until it shone and arranged in a simple style. On her head was a circlet of silk laurel leaves ornamented with emeralds and a dainty necklace of gold and small emeralds shone at her neck.

'Don't she look a bit *odd*?' said Lady Godolphin, walking around Frederica and surveying the finished result. 'The rest will all be in white or pale pastels.'

'She will look *different*,' said Deirdre proudly. 'Where is your fiancé?'

'If you mean Colonel Brian, he's gone off—just like last year's cheese,' sniffed Lady Godolphin. 'Was ever a woman so plagued. Maybe I should not have listened to the gossip from that Lady James creature. She drinks scandal broth for breakfast.'

'Will Lady James be at Almack's?' asked Frederica.

'Not her,' said Lady Godolphin. 'She's person non gracious as far as the patronesses are concerned. We best leave. They don't let anyone in after eleven. I hope you know what you're doing, Deirdre. I think Frederica would have been much better to have borrowed one of my wigs.'

'I am not *bald*,' said the much-goaded Frederica. She longed for the courage to say she did not want to go to Almack's. At least when Martha and Monsieur Andre had finished with her, she felt she looked a nondescript debutante.

Now she felt strange-looking. She would, she was sure, excite the wrong sort of comment. It was all very well for Deirdre with her red hair, slanting green eyes, and modish gowns to excite attention. 'There goes another of the beautiful Armitages,' everyone said when they saw Deirdre, Lady Desire.

And the Duke of Pembury would probably cut her. He would not want to remember he had spent the night with a young miss who looked so *farouche*.

*　　　*　　　*

The Duke of Pembury was leaning against a pillar under the minstrels' gallery at Almack's, wondering whether to go home. It had been a flat, insipid evening. His eyes strayed to the clock. Nearly eleven. There was no sign of Miss Frederica Armitage—which was perhaps just as well. Everyone had been gossiping about the latest Armitage girl, and gossip had it she was sadly plain.

The duke's friend Mr Tommy Ward, a tall, gangling gentleman with sparse hair, a long face and an engaging smile, came strolling up.

'Evening, Robert,' he said, being one of the very few people who had the privilege of addressing the duke by his Christian name. 'You look sadly flat. There are rumours about you flying all over the room. Care to hear a few?'

'No, thank you,' said the duke wearily.

'They're saying you're fishing for a wife,' said Mr Ward blithely. 'They say if you're fishing for a wife then why don't you make the slightest push to dance with anybody? They say there was some scandal about the youngest Armitage, working as a servant in your household so as to entrap you. The mamas say that ain't fair and Miss Armitage should have her vouchers withdrawn. The patronesses refuse to listen but o' course, they're all frightened of Lady Godolphin. I feel quite sorry for the Armitage chit. No one but the most hardened fortune hunter is going to dance with *her*.'

'Do not rattle on so, Tommy. You make my head ache. Frederica Armitage is little more than a schoolgirl. She ran away from her seminary because some trouble at her home was distressing her. She has as much interest in me as I have in her.'

'Why do you not care to dance?'

The duke sighed. 'Truth to tell, Tommy, I find all the ladies here look remarkably the same. Hard to tell one from t'other.'

'Well, by George, if you want an original, take a look at the latest arrival. Reminds me of a sea nymph. She's with Lady Godolphin. Never say *that's* the Armitage girl!'

The duke looked across the bobbing heads of the dancers towards the entrance. Lady Godolphin was outrageously unmistakable. Beside her stood Frederica.

'I believe her eyes are green,' murmured the duke. 'Why did I not notice that before?'

'Only see how they cut her!' exclaimed Mr Ward. 'And she so young and frail. I am going over there this minute . . .'

The duke put a restraining hand on his arm. 'My pleasure, I think, dear Tommy. After all, Miss Armitage and I have already met.'

The duke made his way quickly to where Frederica was now sitting with Lady Godolphin. There was a flush of pink on her cheeks. Frederica had noticed the snubs and wished she could sink through the floor. Beside her, Lady Godolphin was puffing and panting with outrage. Frederica was sure that lady was about to burst out with a string of oaths.

Then she heard that deep, familiar voice. 'I have been looking forward to furthering my acquaintance with Miss Armitage,' said the Duke of Pembury.

Lady Godolphin's wrath disappeared like magic She gave the duke a wide, crocodile-like smile. 'Then I shall leave you with Frederica and go and slay a few gossip-mongers,' she said, rising and shaking out her flimsy skirts.

The duke took her vacated seat. He turned and surveyed Frederica who was nervously playing with the sticks of her fan.

'I compliment you on your appearance, Miss Armitage,' he said.

'It is kind of you to say so,' said Frederica gratefully, 'but I know you are only being kind, Only see how everyone stared at me and then turned their backs. I must look like the veriest freak. I am sure I looked *much* better earlier in the evening, but my sister Deirdre, Lady Harry Desire, she screamed when she saw me and would not let me leave until all the sugar and water had been washed out of my hair.'

The duke laughed. 'Sugar and water? Were they trying to make a pudding of you?'

'No,' confided Frederica naively. 'It was to stick my hair up in curls. But Deirdre said it looked like a wig. If I do not look like a freak *now*, why is everyone being so pointedly cold to me?'

'Because your adventures as a chambermaid are well known.'

'Oh, dear,' said Frederica miserably 'I had not thought of that.' She brightened. 'If I am such a social pariah, there is no point in my remaining in London. I can go home.' Then her face fell. Deirdre had questioned her closely about Sarah and Frederica had told her all about it, believing

Minerva to have read her letter. It was, therefore, no longer a secret. Deirdre had said roundly that of course Papa would not marry Sarah, but now Frederica felt miserably that Papa should do the Right Thing and marry Sarah. It was all so worrying.

'Do not look so distressed,' he said gently. '*My* attentions this evening will bring you back into the fold of the *ton*.'

'Are you so *very* important?' Frederica looked at him curiously.

'In this frivolous world of the top ten thousand,' he said tartly, 'you do not ask a very rich duke of marriageable age whether he is important or not. You are supposed to know better.'

'I will learn,' sighed Frederica. She looked at him cautiously. 'You are much more impressive at Almack's, now I see you set against the other gentlemen.'

'In what way?'

'You are quite elegant,' said Frederica kindly. 'You make every other man in the room seem *fussy*. I would like you to meet my twin brothers, Peregrine and James. They are both suffering from *fashionitis* at the moment and Papa always grumbles about the amount of money they get through, but of course he always pays them because, after all, they are gentlemen and not ladies.'

'And money should not be wasted on ladies?'

'Oh, no. Only just for a Season or two to see if the bait takes. I have great hopes that Papa will despair of me after this Season and will not trouble to try again.'

He looked down with a lurking twinkle in his eyes at the small figure of Frederica sitting next to

107

him. 'I am persuaded, Miss Armitage, that you will have many suitors before the Season is finished. Here comes Lady Godolphin.'

That lady approached them, the blazing candlelight of the ballroom shining right through her dress and exposing not only her corset to the vulgar gaze but a pair of diamonded garters which were holding up her flesh-pink stockings. Following her was a stocky, countrified-looking gentleman.

'This here,' said Lady Godolphin, 'is Mr Harrison who is a friend of your sister Daphne, Mrs Garfield, that is.' Lady Godolphin effected the introductions and Mr Harrison made Frederica a clumsy bow. 'I would be honoured, Miss Armitage,' he said, 'if you would partner me in this next quadrille.'

Frederica's large eyes sparkled with pleasure and she half rose from her seat, but sat down again abruptly as the duke said coldly, 'Apologies, Mr Harrison. The next dance is promised to me.'

Society watched avidly as Mr Harrison bowed again and walked away.

'You do not *have* to dance with me, your grace,' said Frederica. 'Mr Harrison would have done very well.'

'On the contrary,' he said, rising and holding out his arm, 'I wish to dance with you myself.'

Fans fluttered. Eyebrows and quizzing glasses were raised. 'It is just not fair,' said one debutante to another. 'Those wretched Armitage girls! I wonder what Lady James will say when she hears of *this*.'

'Who is this Lady James?' asked her friend.

'You mean you have not heard the *on dits*?' Heads bent close together and tongues wagged.

Lady Godolphin sat with the dowagers and

fanned herself complacently. How little Frederica could dance! Why, the girl was a different person when she danced. What a triumph! If Frederica became a duchess, the Armitage girls, already more famous than the Gurneys, would go down in history.

The elderly Dowager Marchioness of Blessop nudged Lady Godolphin with her elbow. 'Don't see Colonel Brian here tonight. I would have thought your affianced would have escorted you.'

'My fiasco has a great many affairs to attend to,' said Lady Godolphin with great hauteur.

'So I have heard,' cackled the old marchioness. 'And it ain't any use you getting your hopes up about Pembury. Cold fish, that man is.'

'You are a jealous old cat,' said Lady Godolphin. 'And if you don't stow your gab, I'll stuff my reticule right down your scrawny neck.'

Having silenced her companion, Lady Godolphin settled down to watch little Frederica's triumph.

The duke was a leader of fashion. He was a first class sportsman and a notable whip. He belonged neither to the Dandy set nor the Corinthians. Although many members of the demi-monde had found brief favour with him, he had never paid court to any respectable lady, and never before this evening had he singled out any debutante as he had singled out Frederica.

He was enchanted by her dancing and by her youthful manner which was free from missish airs. He had a sudden longing to see her always sparkling and happy the way she now was. He did not want to see her become the crushed and silent Frederica of the house party.

Before the dance was over, Lady Godolphin

109

waddled to her feet to circulate the ballroom and brag quite disgracefully over the size of Frederica's dowry.

By the time the Duke of Pembury led Frederica back to her chair, there was already a large crowd of male admirers waiting to lead her in the next dance.

The Duke of Pembury then proceeded to make it quite plain that he had little interest in any other lady at the assembly. He promptly took his leave.

Despite the fact she was enjoying her newfound social success immensely, Frederica could not help feeling the evening had gone a trifle flat, but she would not admit to herself that the Duke of Pembury's leaving had anything to do with it.

CHAPTER SEVEN

Guy Wentwater called on Lady James two days after the opening ball at Almack's. He no longer entertained any hopes of using her to hurt the Armitages, but he was at loose ends and found Lady James amusing.

Sir Edwin Armitage had sent him an angry letter, saying that if he approached the Hall to try to see Emily again, he would be shot by the gamekeepers as a poacher. The Reverend Charles Armitage had also written to inform Mr Wentwater that his presence in Hopeworth would, in future, be even more unwelcome than it had been hithertofore. The vicar added that it would give him infinite pleasure to horsewhip Mr Wentwater should he dare show his nose near the vicarage again.

110

Since Guy Wentwater did not move in very high circles, he had not heard of Frederica's triumph at the ball, but Lady James most certainly had.

She flew at Guy Wentwater the minute he was ushered in and poured into his willing ears all the gossip she had heard. By now, Lady James had convinced herself that the Duke of Pembury would have married her if only this wretched Armitage girl had not appeared on the scene.

'It is of no use me trying to lure the girl away,' said Mr Wentwater. 'The Armitage sisters will have warned her against me. There must be some way to get at her. Is there anyone of whom she is particularly fond?'

'Let me think.' Lady James strode up and down, the silk of her gown making a swishing noise. 'Lady Godolphin?' she said, coming to a halt.

Mr Wentwater shuddered. 'That horrible old woman would eat us for breakfast. Did Miss Frederica show no evidence of having any school friends?'

'I was not intimate with the chit,' snapped Lady James. 'You must remember when I first met her she was emptying chamber pots. She has the soul of a servant. The minute she was unmasked and hoisted back up into the ranks of the *ton*, her only desire was to have her fellow chambermaid elevated to the rank of lady's maid.'

'Ah, I might do something in that direction,' drawled Guy Wentwater. 'Abduct the maid and the mistress will follow.'

'I do not know what I can do to help,' said Lady James fretfully. 'My name must be kept out of any plot.'

'You must befriend the Armitage chit, find

111

out her movements and get me a description of the maid. I will do the rest. *You* must hint to Pembury that her taste runs to servants and that Miss Frederica is said to be enamoured of some footman.

'If necessary I can produce said footman. We must give Pembury a disgust of the girl for long enough to allow you to do your work—unless, of course, you are over-rating your charms. He may not want you, no matter what happens to Miss Armitage.'

But Lady James's vanity would not allow her to believe that the duke had not one scrap of feeling left for her.

'Do not be insulting,' she said coldly. 'Get rid of Frederica Armitage and leave the rest to me.'

*   *   *

Lady James would have been very surprised if she could have known that the entire Armitage family were determined that Frederica should have nothing to do with the Duke of Pembury. All the sisters had heard of Frederica's evening at Almack's and all were convinced that the duke had been merely amusing himself, but that little Frederica was in danger of losing her heart and spoiling her Season. Deirdre had finally convinced Lady Godolphin of the folly of even thinking of the duke as a possible suitor. The other sisters had also written to her ladyship on the matter. Diana had called on Frederica the day after the ball, prior to journeying to Hopeworth, and had been alarmed by the distinctly dreamy look in her little sister's eyes.

But Frederica had aroused herself from her

dreams enough to give Diana the full story of Sarah Millet, and so it was a very worried Diana who approached the vicarage.

The vicar was at first delighted to see his fox-hunting daughter and was prepared to take her on a tour of the kennels, but his face fell when Diana delivered herself of a long lecture on his morals.

'But Pettifor's going to marry Sarah,' said the vicar, 'so it ain't no use you going on like a jaw-me-dead.'

'Worse and worse,' said Diana severely. 'You constrain that poor man . . .'

'I didn't constrain him,' howled the exasperated vicar. 'He's smelling o' April and May. Can't keep his eyes off the girl. Wants an early marriage.'

'Mr Pettifor!'

'Yes, that long drip o' nothing has blossomed. Got a house out o' me and demanded a mort o' money.'

'Amazing. Where is Sarah?'

'Well, Jimmy Radford said it waren't fitting for her to stay here, so she's lodged with Miss Hamworthy in the village until the wedding, and I've had to pay that old biddy for the housing of her.'

'A small price to pay for having got off marrying the girl yourself,' said Diana dryly.

The vicar raised his eyes to heaven. 'The Lord has forgiven me,' he said piously. "Neither do I condemn thee; go and sin no more." St John, chapter eight . . .'

'Oh, *Papa*. What does Sarah think of all this?'

'Like a dog with two tails. Strutting around the village, bragging 'bout how she's going to be

Mrs Pettifor.'

'The problem does seem to have been resolved,' said Diana doubtfully. 'But trouble of another kind has arisen. Frederica's adventures with the Duke of Pembury have not finished. At her first ball, the duke sat for quite half an hour talking to her, then he danced with her, and then he left, making it quite clear he did not favour any other lady in the room. He was merely amusing himself, but I am afraid little Frederica has taken his attentions seriously. The duke must be dissuaded from paying her any further attention, or we will never get her married. I asked Dantrey to have a word with him, but he merely yawned and said he was much too lazy and for his part he always thought Frederica was a taking little thing. Men! They do stick together.'

'Ever consider Pembury might have a *tendre* for her?'

'Pembury? Nonsense. You have only to look at the man. *You* have met him. He recently had an affair with Lady James, a mature and voluptuous blonde. He is not going to change his exotic tastes and fall in love with a little girl like Frederica. It is your duty, Papa, to write to Lady Godolphin and tell her to make sure Frederica meets as many suitable young men as possible. We are all doing our best. Deirdre sees Frederica almost every day.'

'If you're so anxious, why don't you stay in London and keep an eye on her?' grumbled Mr Armitage.

'I must return to Dantrey. He . . . misses me.' Diana's dark eyes lit up and her whole face seemed to glow.

'You can't leave here so soon,' said the vicar.

'Break your journey for a night.'

But Diana refused to stay.

Before she left Hopeworth, she called on Sarah, and found, to her relief, the maid was much as her father described her. Sarah was already playing the part of the respectable matron and enjoying herself immensely. Mr Pettifor called while Diana was visiting Sarah, and, although he was obviously head over heels in love with the girl, he had also become rather pompous and sanctimonious.

As her carriage finally bore her homewards, Diana resolved to write to Frederica as soon as she arrived. Frederica must know as quickly as possible that the problem of Sarah had finally been resolved.

*   *   *

Contrary to her sisters' fears, Frederica did not think about the Duke of Pembury very much and, like them, was convinced his interest in her at Almack's was based on some fleeting whim.

Unlike her other admirers, he had not called on her the day after the ball, but had sent his servant instead with his card and a bouquet of flowers.

Frederica did not, however, know that he had called two days later, but Lady Godolphin did, and had informed Mice, her butler, to say Miss Armitage was 'not at home'.

The duke accepted the message and was strolling across Hanover Square when he happened for some reason to turn round and look back at the house. He was very surprised to see Frederica at an upstairs window, looking dreamily down into the square. He raised his hand in a salute, but she did not see him.

He walked on his way, puzzled. Never before had he received such a rebuff. People were not in the habit of turning rich and eligible dukes away. After some thought, he decided Lady Godolphin had made a mistake. He let two more days go by and called again. Again he received the same message. He walked away and leaned against the railings of the square. After about ten minutes, a carriage drove up and Lady James alighted. His eyebrows rose in surprise. Lady James, obviously receiving the same rebuff, drove off again. He waited patiently.

Five minutes later, the door opened and Frederica and Lady Godolphin emerged, got into Lady Godolphin's carriage and drove off.

After some thought, he decided to call on his former mistress and find what she was about.

Lady James had just arrived home when he walked up to her home in Curzon Street. She gave him a rapturous welcome. She was looking very beautiful, melting and feminine, and he almost forgot about the ugliness of her character which had only shown through in the latter days of their affair.

After she had fussed over him, plumped cushions behind his back and poured him wine, she proceeded to regale him with the latest gossip. Lord Lascelle's son, Edward, had actually up and married Harriet Wilson's sister. Harriet Wilson was a famous courtesan. Everyone was afraid that Sam Whitbread meant to marry that woman who was living with him. Prinny had let down his belly and wore corsets no more. The old king was dying. Murray, the bookseller, had returned Lord Byron's latest poem to Venice and said he was afraid of

116

publishing it.

'And,' interrupted the duke, 'Lady James has been seen trying to call on Miss Armitage.'

'How people gossip.' Lady James laughed. 'I was merely calling to see how she fared. As a matter of fact, it was because I heard some rather disquieting gossip. It is said she has formed a *tendre* for some *footman*. Not in your household, I trust.'

'Fustian.' His face had gone hard and set.

'Just what I said,' she said quickly. 'I mean, *even* if she took a post as a servant it does not go . . .'

'Exactly,' said the duke. 'I am sure you are too wise, ma'am, to broadcast such a piece of scurrilous gossip yourself. No lady likes to be accused of jealousy.'

'I? Jealous! You are funning.'

He rose to his feet and looked down at her curiously, wondering what he had ever seen in her.

'Good day to you,' he said, turning on his heel.

Lady James made a move as if to run after him, but quickly restrained herself. She would need to be patient and wait—and hope that Guy Wentwater could effect the ruin of Frederica Armitage's reputation.

*   *   *

Guy Wentwater had not been idle. He had been frequenting the taverns and coffee houses favoured by the servants of the *ton*. He was searching for a good-looking footman who liked gambling too much. After a week of searching, he struck gold. His prey was William Richards, second footman in Lord Cooper's town house in Mayfair. Richards was a tall, engaging young man, handsome in his pink and silver livery. Introducing himself as a Mr Jackson, Guy Wentwater soon became on friendly terms with the footman. Their friendship proceeded rapidly through several bottles of wine to several games of hazard. The unfortunate Richards did not know that the dice were literally loaded against him, and found with a sobering shock that he owed his newfound friend one hundred guineas—a sum it would take him several years to pay back.

Embarrassed and miserable, he stammered out a plea for time to pay.

Guy Wentwater leaned back in his chair and smiled lovingly on the blushing footman. 'I could forget about your debt, my boy,' he said, 'if you would but render me a trifling service.'

'Anything,' babbled the unfortunate Richards.

'Then lean your head close to mine for I do not wish to be overheard. Good. This then is what you must do . . .'

*   *   *

Perhaps the Duke of Pembury might never have been able to call on Frederica had Lady Godolphin resumed amicable relations with Colonel Brian. But when there appeared to be no sign of a reconciliation on the horizon, Lady Godolphin decided that drastic measures must be taken to restore her beauty.

Firstly, Martha, her lady's maid, was told to prepare a 'cosmetic bath'. Baths were usually medicinal or cosmetic. No one really bothered taking them for simple dreary reasons of cleanliness. Lady Godolphin's bath was to consist of two pounds of barley meal, eight pounds of bran, and a quantity of borage leaves boiled up in spring water.

Secondly, Mary was despatched to the City in a hack to fetch a tincture for the teeth from Greenough's apothecary shop near St Sepulchre's, Lady Godolphin claiming that her usual home-made mixture of the ashes of nettles, tobacco and honey was doing nothing to whiten her remaining teeth. Greenough's tinctures claimed not only to keep the teeth white but to 'perfectly cure the scurvy of the gums, fasten and preserve the teeth, render them white and beautiful, and prevent them decaying and keep such as are decayed from becoming worse'.

So it was when the Duke of Pembury called again that Lady Godolphin was lying abovestairs in a bath which looked like porridge. Mice had not been given instructions to refuse the duke admittance. On the previous two occasions Lady Godolphin had been told of the duke's arrival and had sent Mice back with the 'not home' message. But Lady Godolphin quite often told callers she was not at home because she simply could not be bothered entertaining them.

Mice therefore informed Frederica of the duke's arrival and Frederica promptly told Mice to show the duke into the drawing room.

Since Frederica had not thought too much about the Duke of Pembury during the past days, she was not prepared for her own odd reaction at the sight of him. Her breathing became rapid and she could hardly bring herself to look at him. She had been escorted here and there by various admirers and not one of them had caused her to feel any social unease.

The fickle spring weather had turned chilly and the duke was wearing a long black wool cloak lined with red silk and fastened with gold frogs. His calfskin boots, polished to a mirror shine, were worn over tight pantaloons of drab kerseymere. The femininity of his ruffled shirt emphasized the rather harsh masculinity of his face.

The duke was relieved to find Miss Armitage looking much the way she had done at Hatton Abbey. The sea nymph of the ball had disappeared. Her half-dress was of silk, and very fashionable, being intricately plated on the bosom and falling to four deep flounces at the hem. But the pale violet colour of the gown did not flatter Frederica.

Frederica waited until the tea tray had been brought in before asking him politely how he was.

'Very well, Miss Armitage,' said the duke, crossing his legs and surveying her curiously. 'I had begun to wonder whether you had taken me in dislike. I called twice before and each time was refused admittance.'

'I cannot understand why,' said Frederica. 'It was none of my doing. I did not think dukes were refused admittance anywhere.'

'Where is Lady Godolphin?'

'My lady is in the bath.'

'You amaze me. Are you enjoying your first Season?'

'Ye-es,' said Frederica doubtfully. 'I am a trifle fatigued. We go to many balls and parties. I am beginning to think perhaps that arranged marriages might be a very good thing.'

'Indeed! But that way you may end up with some gentleman who displeases you.'

'I think I may very well end up with some gentleman who does not precisely make my heart beat faster,' said Frederica. 'It is done, you know . . . ladies marry just anyone. Only very, very rich families can afford more than one Season.'

'With so many gentlemen about, I am sure you will find yourself attracted to at least one of them.'

'Perhaps. It is not like books, is it?' Frederica giggled. 'I cannot imagine anyone turning pale with passion at the sight of me.'

He suddenly frowned and Frederica wondered whether she had offended him. But the duke was remembering that one kiss. He had never before experienced anything like it. If only he could try again to prove to himself that his own strong feelings had been brought on by the strangeness of the situation he had found himself in.

His eyes fell to her mouth. It was very well-shaped. Amazing girl! Not at all attractive taken as a whole, but when studied closely, one discovered many beauties.

Her large eyes were very expressive, her ankles were neat, and her movements graceful,

'Did I say something wrong?' asked Frederica nervously.

'No,' he said. 'I was merely wondering whether you were going to offer me any of that tea.'

Frederica blushed. Hurriedly, she poured tea and offered cakes. She racked her brains for something to say. The drawing room was well-proportioned but it seemed to have become small and airless and charged with electricity, as if a thunderstorm were about to break.

'I think the pleasantest outing I had,' she said, 'was to Hyde Park. The deer are so very tame they let you stroke their antlers. It was almost like being in the country again. Oh, I know it is not fashionable to prefer the country, but London seems so very enclosed. So many buildings and so many don'ts.'

'Don'ts?'

'There are all the people one must not recognize and all the places a lady must not go, like St James's Street and Bond Street. It is forbidden to show any excess of emotion, to laugh or to cry. I found the opera most affecting the other night and started to cry, and even Lady Godolphin was appalled and it takes a great deal to upset *her*.'

'Do not despise the conventions.' He smiled. 'They are in their way protection for you. They prevent a young miss from being subjected to over-warm attentions from her gallants.'

Frederica sighed. 'I find it a very unsatisfactory way of life. I enjoyed working as a chambermaid.'

'My dear Miss Armitage, pray do not go about saying such things. The very fact that you *were* a chambermaid nearly ruined you socially.'

'And if it had not been for the gallantry of the Duke of Pembury at Almack's, I am persuaded I should still be out of favour. I have had a letter from my sister, Diana, Lady Dantrey. She tells me that the problems at home which had distressed me so much are now resolved. I am glad, but, on the other hand, it makes it so very tempting to prove myself a failure so that I might return and forget about all this nonsense.' Frederica waved an eloquent little hand, expressively damning all the fashionable world and its foibles from Grosvenor Square to St James's.

How easy it was to talk to him, thought

Frederica. Then she remembered the lectures she had received from Lady Godolphin and Deirdre. The duke was merely amusing himself. She must not take him seriously. But he was by far the most exciting man she had ever met.

'Do you go to the Coopers' ball tonight?' he asked.

'Yes. I do not know which gown to wear. I now have *five*, one from each sister.'

'What colours are these gowns?'

'Let me see. Two white, one pink, one primrose, and one blue.'

'What colour of blue?' he asked, remembering how blue her eyes had looked when she smiled.

'Like a summer sky.' Frederica smiled. 'Deirdre, Lady Desire, insists it is just the thing.'

'Who chose the gown you were wearing at Almack's?'

'Deirdre.'

'Then be guided by Deirdre. You need colour.'

'I know,' said Frederica wistfully.

All of a sudden, he wanted to reassure her, to tell her he found her beautiful no matter what she wore. He was startled at the intensity of his feelings.

There came a great thumping and crashing and swearing from abovestairs. Lady Godolphin was obviously emerging from her bath.

He felt he could not bear any of Lady Godolphin's vulgar company. He rose to his feet to take his leave and Frederica rose at the same time, her fingers nervously pleating the silk of her gown.

'You should wear something warmer,' he found himself saying. 'This room is cold.'

Frederica once again found his presence and nearness overwhelming and wished he would go. 'I have a shawl somewhere,' she said, looking around the room in a vague way.

He put his hat and gloves down again on a console table.

'Miss Armitage,' he said, 'do you remember that I kissed you?'

Wide startled eyes flew to his face. 'You did not!' gasped Frederica.

He smiled. 'You were asleep in my arms in that hut.' Frederica remembered her dream and a tide of red flooded her cheeks. 'You had better go,' she said in a little voice.

He leaned forward to retrieve his hat and gloves. Then he straightened up, threw his hat and gloves on to the sofa, and jerked Frederica into his arms.

She was too startled to struggle, and, before she knew it, he had covered her mouth with his own. She stayed very still in his embrace. She felt warm and protected and isolated from all the troubles of the world. But then the warm safe feeling went away as a dizzying passion rose up in her. Frightened and alarmed, Frederica wrenched herself out of his arms. She was very white.

'Please leave,' she whispered.

She looked so young and dazed and shaken, he felt like some horrible satyr. He wanted to say he loved her, but he was frightened it would turn out to be untrue.

So, instead, he said the worst thing he could possibly have said. 'I am sorry,' said the Duke of Pembury. 'I must have had too much to drink. Please forgive me and do put the unfortunate incident from your mind.'

'Go *away!*' said Frederica.

And to add insult to injury—he did!

Mary decided to walk back from the City to the West End. To a country girl, it was no very great distance and it seemed almost immoral to waste a shilling on a smelly hackney carriage.

She stood outside the apothecary shop, tucking the bottle of tincture into her apron pocket. Walking would give her an opportunity to look at the shops. It was then she heard her name, and, looking up, saw Lady James leaning out of a carriage window, beckoning to her.

Mary was unaware that Lady James had followed her from Hanover Square. She did not want to speak to Lady James but was too frightened to refuse.

Mary approached the carriage and bobbed a curtsy. 'I recognized you,' said Lady James, smiling sweetly. She held open the carriage door. 'Are you returning to the West End?'

'Yes, my lady,' stammered Mary, quite overwhelmed. Her new status as lady's maid, she decided, must have elevated her amazingly in Lady James's eyes.

Once inside the carriage, Mary found herself subject to the full battery of Lady James's charm.

She was asked her impressions of London and listened to as if she were the wisest sage.

When they were bowling along Oxford Street, Lady James said, 'Pray do not tell Miss Armitage of our meeting. I am afraid Lady Godolphin does not like me. Promise, now!'

'I promise, my lady,' said Mary, dazzled and enchanted by this new, charming Lady James.

'I also wish to discuss a little matter with you. It will be a secret between ourselves. Can you come to my home at 9 Curzon Street next Wednesday?'

'I could try,' said Mary, intrigued and excited. 'But what will I tell Miss Armitage?'

'We will not tell her anything,' said Lady James, bestowing a warm smile on Mary and squeezing her hand. 'If you call at ten in the morning, Lady Godolphin and Miss Armitage will still be asleep and there will be no reason to lie. I do so *hate* lies.'

Mary nodded fervently and was still beaming and nodding when she was set down at the corner of Hanover Square.

'Ugly little thing,' thought Lady James contemptuously as her carriage rolled on. 'I may not need to use her if Wentwater is clever with this footman business But . . . we shall see.'

*   *   *

The Duke of Pembury strode into Hubbold's coffee house, scowling like a demon.

'You look the way I feel,' grinned his friend Mr Tommy Ward. 'Hock and seltzer is the answer.'

'The trouble is neither in my head nor in my spleen,' said the duke, sitting down opposite Mr Ward.

'Aha! Then it is your heart. Still pining after Miss Armitage?'

The duke looked at his friend in amazement. 'What on earth gave you such a chuckle-headed idea as that?'

'Stands to reason. Made a dead set for the girl at Almack's. Never seen you look so interested in any female. Come in here looking like thunder.

Love takes men odd ways. Some get all happy and smiling and some, like you, go around cursing and kicking the cat.'

'I am not in love with Miss Armitage or anyone else,' said the duke in frigid accents. 'Pray let us talk about something sensible.'

'As you wish,' said Mr Ward amiably. 'Feather-head is running at Newmarket, Humphrey's filly, and I'll lay you a monkey she comes in first.'

The two men conversed amiably on sporting topics, but all the time he was chatting, the duke's brain was working feverishly.

Love? Was that what ailed him? Love was supposed to be a pleasant emotion, not this puzzled mixture of bafflement and yearning.

He would go to the Coopers' ball. The sooner he saw Frederica Armitage again the better. He would no doubt find her just an ordinary, colourless little girl who had briefly caught his attention.

CHAPTER EIGHT

Lord and Lady Cooper lived in great style in Grosvenor Square. Lady James arrived early. Despite the fact she was not welcome at such austere places as Almack's or the Italian opera, most other doors were open to her. She only regretted Guy Wentwater was such bad *ton* he was not invited to the Coopers'. She would need to perform her part in the plan and trust he had done his.

Although her reputation was low with the ladies,

127

the gentlemen still flocked about her, begging her to dance. Lady James flirted, danced and chatted, all the while keeping a sharp eye on the door to note the arrival of Miss Armitage.

At last Frederica was there, looking well enough in a simple blue gown and a fine sapphire necklace, but nothing out of the common way, thought Lady James complacently, and then wondered if all the plotting and planning were a waste of time. Such as Frederica Armitage could never hope to attract a high stickler like the Duke of Pembury.

But fifteen minutes later, Lady James found that the irritating Miss Armitage had undergone a transformation. Her eyes glowed like the sapphires around her neck. Her whole slim body seemed to radiate with vitality. It was then Lady James noticed the Duke of Pembury had arrived.

Despite her appearance, Frederica was finding the duke's presence in the ballroom an agony. She was terrified he might approach her, and at the same time, she was terrified he might not.

She found Lady Godolphin was over at the far corner of the room and decided to seek sanctuary in the shadow of that formidable lady's bulk. As she edged through the crowd of people around the dance floor, she felt a note being pressed into her hand. She looked about, but could not even begin to guess who had given her the note.

Frederica retired behind a pillar out of the crush and spread open the paper. 'Miss Armitage,' she read, 'I am only a lowly servant in this establishment, but I am in sore trouble and need your help. If you could be of service, ask the tall footman by the East Door to guide you to me. I am desperate. Yr. Humble Servant.'

Frederica was very much a daughter of the vicarage. She barely paused to think about the wisdom of answering the note's summons. Someone needed her help.

She made her way to the east door and showed the note to a tall, handsome footman. 'This way, miss,' he said without so much as the flicker of an eyelid.

Frederica followed his tall figure along a passage which led away from the ballroom. He opened the door of a small morning room and ushered her inside.

'Where is this servant?' demanded Frederica.

'It is I, Miss Armitage,' said William Richards. He was glad she was such a small, slight-looking lady. All he wanted to do was get his part in this comedy over with as quickly as possible. His gambling debts weighed heavy on his mind.

'You?' said Frederica. 'How did you come to hear of me?'

'It is well known you have a kind heart, Miss Armitage.'

Frederica was suddenly aware she was alone with this young man. The faint strains of a waltz came from the ballroom.

'Tell me Mr . . .?'

'Richards, ma'am.'

'Tell me, Mr Richards, what is your problem?' To Frederica's alarm, the tall footman fell on one knee in front of her.

'*You* are,' he said. 'Oh, Miss Armitage. I *love* you.'

*   *   *

129

'Looking for Miss Armitage?' Lady James's mocking voice sounded in the Duke of Pembury's ear.

'Good evening, Lady James,' he said. 'I trust you are no longer spreading false rumours about Miss Armitage's devotion to some footman.'

'I did not start the gossip. The silly girl has, however, gone too far. She is with him now.'

'Where?' The duke looked first one way and then the other.

'Come with me and I will show you. I feel perhaps you should caution her on her behaviour.'

The duke sighed. He felt sure Lady James was simply trying to get him alone to enact a scene. But it might be better to depress her ambitions for once and for all.

'Lead on,' he said amiably. 'I will follow.'

Lady James led the way out of the ballroom by the east door. She hoped Guy Wentwater's creature had managed to get the timing right. It would be fatal to burst in just as Miss Armitage was soundly slapping some footman's face.

But Richards was determined to play his part right. He was not going to touch Miss Armitage until he heard voices in the passage outside.

'In here, I think,' he heard Lady James say.

He had been standing with bowed head before Frederica who had been reading him a stern lecture on his folly, but at the sound of Lady James's voice, he leapt into action.

Frederica, who considered the young man well and truly cowed, suddenly found herself enfolded in a fight embrace.

'I love you madly,' said Richards in a loud voice, just as the door opened.

130

Lady James smiled with satisfaction.

The Duke of Pembury saw the passionate scene and then a red mist of rage rose before his eyes. He took hold of the footman by the shoulder, swung him about, dragged Frederica out of his arms and jerked her violently away so that she hurtled into the corner of the room. Then he smashed his fist full and hard right on the point of Richards's chin. The footman stretched his length on the floor. Lady James began to scream as loudly as possible. It was part of Wentwater's plan to have as many witnesses to Frederica's unfortunate 'infatuation' as possible.

The note that Frederica had shown Richards lay on the floor. The duke picked it up and read it, and then he raised his eyes and looked long and thoughtfully at Lady James. 'Say anything, madam,' he grated, 'and I will expose your plot.'

The guests came crowding in at the doorway demanding to know what all the fuss was about.

The duke moved quickly and put his arm about Frederica who had just risen shakily to her feet.

'I am afraid you have arrived at the end of this comedy of errors,' he said. 'Miss Armitage had retired from the ballroom to try to remove a speck of soot from her eye. Lady James told me of Miss Armitage's whereabouts, knowing I was looking for her. This unfortunate footman was endeavouring to help Miss Armitage, but I am afraid my jealousy got the better of me, and I rendered the poor man unconscious before I learned the truth of the matter.

'You must forgive me. It is not every day I become engaged to be married.'

'Married!' screamed Lady James.

'Married?' whispered Frederica, trying to move

away from the duke, but his arm was like an iron band about her waist.

'Married!' screamed Lady Godolphin, using her elbows as battering rams to force a way to the front. 'Oh, joy. Oh, rupture!'

The duke bowed to Lady Godolphin. 'I must apologise for being so impetuous. I will call on you tomorrow, my lady, to obtain your kind permission to pay my addresses.'

Richards gave a groan and tried to struggle into an upright position. 'Leave me with this poor man,' said the duke. 'You, too, Lady James. I must make my amends.'

He pushed everyone out of the room and then said to Frederica, 'Look happy and we will come about with your reputation intact.'

'Why did you say we were to be married?' asked Frederica.

'Hush. Later. Go now and leave me with this fellow.' Frederica walked back to the ballroom in a daze. The duke grasped the footman firmly by his cravat and heaved him up on to a chair. Richards groaned and clutched his head.

The duke poured a glass of brandy from a decanter on a side table and held it to the footman's lips. 'Drink this,' he snapped.

Richards took a great gulp, and then choked and shuddered.

'Now,' said the duke, holding up the note. 'What is the meaning of this?'

Richards thought as quickly as his bewildered senses and aching head would allow him. If he betrayed 'Mr Jackson' then Mr Jackson would demand to be paid.

'I have behaved like a fool,' said Richards. 'I fell

in love with Miss Armitage. There had been talk of her being a servant herself, and I was crazy enough to hope . . .'

'Come, man, tell the truth. What part did Lady James play in this?'

Richards looked genuinely puzzled. He had never heard of Lady James. He had merely been told to spring into action when he heard a woman's voice outside the room.

'Nothing,' he said. 'I have never spoken to Lady James.'

It was the duke's turn to look puzzled. 'What happened between you and Miss Armitage?' he demanded.

'She was giving me a lecture and I just lost my head and seized her. Oh, what am I to do? I must have been mad.'

The duke experienced a certain fellow feeling. After all, look how the sight of Frederica in another man's arms had driven *him* mad.

'I cannot go back on my explanation for the reason you and Miss Armitage were closeted together,' said the duke. 'You must promise me you will never approach her again.'

'Yes, your grace,' said Richards fervently. 'Never, ever.'

'Very well. You may go.'

'Thank you, your grace. May I offer your grace my congratulations?'

'Congratulations? Oh, yes, that,' said the duke, realizing to his amazement that he had in fact proposed to Frederica Armitage.

Lady James was waiting nervously for the duke in the passage outside. She was prepared to lie, to tell all about Guy Wentwater in order to escape

133

censure.

But the duke smiled on her vaguely and said, 'I am sorry. I jumped to a wrong conclusion. It seems this footman was enamoured of Miss Armitage and lost his head. We will maintain the fiction, however, that he was helping her remove a speck from her eye.'

Lady James wanted to accuse Frederica, to say that no doubt Frederica had encouraged the footman, but she knew she would not be believed. She could only be thankful Richards had held his tongue. If Richards had told the duke Guy Wentwater had coerced him into trying to ruin Frederica, then she herself would become part of that plot.

'I am glad I am proved innocent,' she said lightly. 'No reputations ruined. As it turns out, you had no need to propose to the girl. I do not think she believed you in any case, so a simple statement to . . .'

'But I *am* going to marry her,' said the duke, feeling light-hearted. 'By Jove, that footman did me a very great favour. He made up my mind for me.'

He walked away, leaving Lady James consumed with fury. Portly old Lord George Southern wheezed along the passage in Lady James's direction. 'Ah, there you are.' He grinned. 'Been lookin' for you. Hear you're on the market.'

'I beg your pardon,' said Lady James, hardly able to believe her ears. Lord Southern slid an arm about her waist. 'Hear you're all finished with Pembury. What about me, heh?'

Tears of rage started to Lady James's eyes. She longed to smack Lord Southern's leering face, but that would cause a scene. She jerked herself free and walked into the ballroom, two spots of colour burning on her cheeks.

Frederica Armitage was the centre of attention. She was standing next to Lady Godolphin while members of society milled about, each anxious to compliment the future Duchess of Pembury.

Respectable Miss Armitage. So near social ruin, and now, so far.

Mad jealousy seized Lady James by the throat, almost causing her to choke. She began to notice the sly, furtive looks being cast in her direction. Malicious London society was obviously wondering how she was taking the news of her ex-lover's engagement.

Pinning a bright smile on her face, she contrived to be at her gayest and most charming, although anger burned in her heart and her head ached abominably.

Frederica also had a fixed smile on her face. She was grateful to the duke for having rescued her from an embarrassing situation. She was confident he would manage to disengage himself from her with his usual aplomb the following day. Her eyes kept straying to his tall figure. He looked very much at ease.

He came up, to her as soon as the waltz was announced and her small court of admirers fell back to allow him to lead her to the floor.

'So, my love,' he said, smiling down at her, 'do you like the idea of an early wedding?'

Frederica tripped over his feet, apologised, and then looked up at him with wide, desperate eyes. 'But you only said that about us being engaged . . . to save me from an awful situation.'

'So I did,' he agreed. 'But having said it, I find

135

I like the idea more and more. Tell me about the footman.'

'It is all very odd,' said Frederica a little breathlessly, for the pressure of his hand on her waist was doing odd things to her nervous system. 'I received the note and immediately went to see if I could be of help.

'He seemed to be genuinely regretting his rash action. He was standing before me with his head bowed, and then, as soon as he heard someone in the passage outside, he . . . he grabbed me.'

The duke frowned. Yet Richards had been very convincing . . .

'Do not answer any more mysterious summonses without consulting me,' he said.

She shook her head. 'Do you *really* want to marry me?' she asked.

'Yes, really.'

'Why?'

'You kiss like an angel.'

'Oh,' said Frederica dismally. 'Perhaps I might get used to it.'

'You had better. For I am determined to marry you.'

Frederica gave a nervous little laugh. Was love like this? Terrified of someone and yet, at the same time, terrified of losing him?

*   *   *

News of his daughter's moment of glory had not yet reached the Reverend Charles Armitage. He was enjoying his own moment of glory.

Hounds were streaming out before him in full cry. Mr Armitage was sure the old dog fox that had plagued him for so long was near the end of its mangy days. All day long he had hunted it. For two whole hours, hounds had lost the scent but now they were on to the fox again. 'Tally-ho! Hoop! Hoop! Hoop!' roared the vicar.

'That's him, all right,' screamed the vicar to John Summer who was acting as whipper-in. He spurred his mount up a big backed hill and raced down the other side.

'Dang me, but I'll be in at the death this time,' muttered the vicar. 'They have him, by George!'

The exhausted fox was lying still, surrounded by a circle of howling, baying hounds.

The excited vicar hurtled from his saddle and, diving into their midst, seized the fox by the scruff and held it high.

'Lookee,' he cried to the grinning John. 'I'll break his neck, take the brush and pads, and you jolly boys,' said the vicar, beaming down at his hounds, 'can have the rest.'

'Papa!' A scream borne on the wind. *'Papa!'* Louder now.

The vicar stood with his mouth open, the limp, exhausted fox still held high above his head.

His daughter Diana who lived over on the far side of Hopeminster at the old Osbadiston place came riding up.

'Papa!' she shouted. 'I have just had an express from Deirdre. Frederica is engaged to the Duke of Pembury!'

'My little Frederica a duchess?' Tears started to the vicar's eyes. He hugged the fox to his bosom and walked across to Diana who was dismounting. 'Here, John,' said the vicar over his shoulder, 'call off them damn hounds. Can't hear a word. Now,

Diana, are you sure?'

'Here is Deirdre's letter. See, she says . . . oh, Papa, you have finally caught old Reynard.'

Diana loved hunting but hated the kill. 'Hey, what?' The vicar looked down at the fox in his arms in a bemused way. His Frederica a duchess! He felt a great rush of gratitude.

'Give me that animal,' said Diana impatiently, 'and take the letter.'

The vicar handed over the fox like someone moving in a dream. He read Deirdre's letter over and over again.

He heard a hoarse cry from John Summer and looked up.

Diana was riding off like the wind, the fox tucked under one arm.

'Come back here!' yelled the vicar, jumping up and down with rage.

Diana rode on until she felt the fox begin to struggle in the crook of her arm. She reined in her horse and threw the fox on the ground.

'Off with you, Reynard,' said Diana cheerfully. 'You have earned your freedom.'

She waited while the fox, recovering its wind and energy, loped off into the bushes.

The Reverend Charles Armitage was left prey to wildly conflicting emotions. 'My fox . . . gone. My daughter . . . a duchess,' he kept saying, over and over again.

But finally, joy at Frederica's success soon outweighed anger at the escape of his old enemy. He reminded himself of all the famous days of sport the old fox had provided, and set out to tell Squire Radford of Frederica's triumph.

138

CHAPTER NINE

It was perhaps unfortunate that the Duke of Pembury had never before courted a respectable young girl. He was anxious not to frighten his virginal bride-to-be with any further show of passion, and so he was correct and formal in his behaviour in the days following the Coopers' ball.

He was extremely proud of his conduct and would have been amazed had he known that what he considered his excellent manner and address were only making him seem cold and reserved in Frederica's eyes.

Frederica felt she had no one in whom she could confide. Her sisters were all so excited and delighted with her success that she could not bring herself to tell any one of them of her fears and doubts.

Two of her former school 'friends' had paid calls, but they had laughed and chattered about clothes and beaux and had so patently envied Frederica her good fortune that she cringed from saying anything other than that she was 'delighted' with the engagement.

Debutantes were not supposed to addle their brains with missish doubts about love and affection. The suitor's status and income were all that mattered. To voice any doubts whatsoever would cause one to be damned as an Original.

Frederica searched the duke's face in vain for any signs of that mocking tenderness she had seen there before.

She did at last confide in Mary, but Mary only

looked puzzled. If Miss Frederica did not want to wed the Duke of Pembury, then she surely only had to say so—not understanding how hard it was for Frederica even to think of objecting to the engagement when presents and congratulations arrived by every post.

Despite her fears, Frederica could not help enjoying her success. It *was* pleasant to find she was about to enter the most successful marriage of all the Armitage girls. When she was not with the duke, Frederica found she could easily bask in the envy and admiration of society. But when he was with her, chilly and correct, he seemed like a frightening stranger.

Mary had not forgotten her appointment with Lady James. On the Wednesday, a week after the Coopers' ball, Mary walked through the quiet morning streets from Hanover Square to Curzon Street. She stood outside the tall house for several moments, debating whether to march boldly up to the front door, or whether to go down the area steps to the kitchen.

Then she reminded herself she was calling on the mistress of the house and boldly marched up the marble steps and performed a lively tattoo on the brass knocker.

A tall, grim-looking butler answered the summons and said he doubted my lady was at home, implying that my lady would naturally not be at home to such an undistinguished creature as Mary.

Mary flashed him a look of triumph when he came back and announced that Lady James would be 'delighted' to see her.

Mary was ushered into a pretty morning room.

'Sit down, my dear,' cooed Lady James. 'You are a good girl and did not forget our appointment. You did not tell anyone about it?'

'Not me,' said Mary stoutly.

'Good. Now before we discuss my little problem, you must take some hot chocolate to warm you. Ah, me. How I long for the summer. Do you go to Brighton?'

She poured a large cup of steaming hot chocolate and handed it to Mary. 'I do not know my mistress's plans,' said Mary, 'I have never seen the sea.'

'Oh, it is wonderful at Brighton. So invigorating. And the Pavilion! Just like an Oriental palace.'

Mary took a gulp of the chocolate. 'You wanted to discuss something with me, my lady?' she ventured timidly.

'Later,' said Lady James airily. 'Your mistress must be in alt over her engagement.'

'Yes, my lady,' said Mary, and blinked her eyelids rapidly to bring the room into focus. How warm it had become, and how dizzy she felt. She took another gulp of chocolate to try to revive herself, but only succeeded in feeling dizzier than ever.

'Perhaps our dear Miss Armitage is not the innocent she seems?' Lady James's face began to swim before Mary's eyes.

'I beg your pardon . . .' she began, and then slid from the shiny striped satin of the sofa on which she was sitting on to the floor.

Lady James rose briskly to her feet. She leaned down and prised open one of Mary's eyes. 'Out cold,' she muttered with satisfaction. 'Time to summon Miss Armitage. Wentwater should be here shortly. I have need of him.'

*   *   *

Frederica Armitage had had to dress herself. Mary, it transpired, was nowhere to be found. She supposed the maid was out and about, looking in all the shop windows from Oxford Street to Holborn.

Mice, the butler, scratched at the door and called out that a messenger from the Duke of Pembury was waiting below.

Frederica hurried down to the hall. There was a large, burly man in footman's livery waiting by the door.

'The message is for you personal, miss,' he said with a look at Mice who was hovering by the green baize door which led down to the kitchens.

'Follow me,' said Frederica, leading the way into the sparse cold reception room to the left of the hall which Lady Godolphin only used to interview tradespeople or entertain members of society whom she did not like.

'Now, what is this message?' demanded Frederica, shutting the door.

'Your maid, Mary, has been arrested for stealing. I only said I was from the duke. You're to come with me 'fore she's taken to Newgate.'

'But that is ridiculous,' gasped Frederica. 'Mary would not steal anything.'

'The constable says if you was to say a word for her, then he'll release her.'

'Of course,' said Frederica. 'I will give you a note . . . no . . . I will come myself. Wait here until I fetch my bonnet.'

'Is anything the matter, miss?' demanded Mice suspiciously as Frederica was making her way out the front door with the messenger.

142

'No, no,' said Frederica. 'Mary is in a little trouble.'

'Then I will send two of the footmen . . .'

'That will not be necessary,' said Frederica hurriedly, not wishing any of Lady Godolphin's servants to witness Mary's humiliation.

'Where is she?' asked Frederica as the footman led the way across Hanover Square. 'Is it far? Perhaps I should have taken the carriage.'

'Only as far as Curzon Street,' said the man.

'Oh, then, I can easily walk there. Tell me more about it.'

'I haven't the rights of it,' said the man stolidly. 'Better for you to see for yourself, miss.'

Puzzled and anxious, Frederica hurried after him. Although she was very worried about Mary, she was also worried about this messenger. When Mice had offered the escort of two footmen, she could have sworn he looked apprehensive.

The man eventually halted outside a house in Curzon Street. 'Your maid's held in there, miss,' he said.

'Who lives here?' demanded Frederica.

'Blessed if I know, miss.'

'Then who sent you?'

'Don't you want to help Mary?' said the man coaxingly. 'If you go inside they'll answer all your questions. The constable is there and the watch. Mary's crying something cruel.'

All her doubts about the messenger forgotten, Frederica picked up her skirts and ran lightly up the steps. The door opened before she had time to knock. She nodded to the butler and walked past him into the hall.

And stopped dead in her tracks.

Standing facing her was a man she remembered well. The last time she had seen him was when he was sitting with her family in the vicarage at the supper table all those years ago It had been hoped he would marry Annabelle. He had made jokes about his work, saying he traded in black ivory. It was the vicar who had enlightened the family by explaining grimly that 'black ivory' meant slaves and that Mr Wentwater was a slave trader.

'You!' said Frederica.

And then a savage blow on the head struck her down from behind.

'Very good, Giles,' said Guy Wentwater as Lady James came hurrying out of her drawing room and screamed at the sight of Frederica's unconscious body sprawled on the tiled floor of the hall.

'You have surely not killed her!' said Lady James. 'I said there was to be no killing.'

'Do not worry,' said Guy Wentwater. He turned to the footman. 'Tie her up, and her maid, and we'll get them into the carriage after dark.'

Lady James shivered. 'Where are you taking them?'

'To the Humes' mansion on the Richmond Road. I took the lease of it for a year in your name. Remember, my lady, it is also up to you to pay the guards handsomely for a year if you want these women kept alive . . . If you want them kept alive.'

'Of course,' said Lady James, wringing her hands. 'I wonder whether we should keep her away that long. What will become of me when they are finally released?'

'By your own reckoning,' drawled Guy Wentwater, 'you will be the Duchess of Pembury by that time. You have a whole year in which to entrap

144

Pembury and a whole year to think up explanations. I can ship them to America if you like.'

'Perhaps that might be best,' said Lady James, hugging herself and wondering if she would ever feel warm again. 'What is the next part of the plan?'

'If you told me the right story, then young Frederica makes a habit of running away. Write a letter, supposed to come from her, and send it to Pembury. Say she is running away because she can't stand the idea of marriage to him.

'His pride will prevent him from trying to seek her out.'

'His pride might prevent him from accepting the fact she has run away,' said Lady James. 'Faith, 'tis cold.'

*   *   *

The duke's first reaction to the letter, received the following day, that was supposed to come from Frederica was a kind of sad acceptance. Ever since the announcement of the engagement, Frederica had been quiet and withdrawn and had seemed scared of him. He had been carefully formal and correct, and yet the better he had, in his own eyes, behaved towards her, the more frightened she had become.

He called at Lady Godolphin's to wearily present his compliments to Miss Armitage and to tell her that he had agreed to the termination of their engagement.

The house was in an uproar. Deirdre, Lady Desire, was there; her eyes red with weeping. Lady Godolphin was lumbering up and down like a hippopotamus, wailing that Frederica had taken leave of her senses.

'I *am* sorry I have driven her to such extreme measures . . .' began the duke.

But Deirdre interrupted him with a cry of, 'I am frightened. Just look at this letter. It is misspelt. This is not Frederica's handwriting.'

'Let me see it,' said the duke.

Lady Godolphin handed him a letter. 'Dear Lady Godolphin,' he read. 'I don't want to marry Penbury, and so I am running away to where you cant find me and make me marry him. I am distresed and misarable. Forgive me. F.'

The duke took out his quizzing glass and studied the letter and then he slowly lifted it to his nose and sniffed. A faint odour of violets came from the paper. On paper such as this had his ex-mistress Lady James, written him many a letter. Not that she had ever written him love letters, only demands that he pay her dressmaker's bills.

'What a fool I am!' he cried. 'That footman . . . and I believed him! Do not fear, ladies. I hope to restore Frederica to you very soon.'

He rushed from the house, leaving Lady Godolphin and Deirdre staring after him.

'Beg pardon, my lady,' said Mice. 'I did try to tell you, but you wasn't listening. This strange footman called, saying he had a message for Miss Armitage from the Duke of Pembury. Then she says as she is leaving with this man that Mary is in a little trouble. Perhaps Mary was paid to lure her away.'

He had the satisfaction of seeing his mistress go into strong hysterics before he descended to the kitchen to tell the staff that that would teach old 'boot face' to listen to him next time.

Meanwhile, the duke called first at Lady James's

mansion and found her absent. He promptly headed for Grosvenor Square and startled Lord and Lady Cooper by demanding to see their footman, Richards.

Left alone with Richards, the duke said in a deceptively mild voice, 'I think you have something to tell me about Miss Armitage.'

'No, sir,' said Richards, all innocence.

'Then perhaps this will refresh your memory, young man,' said the duke, punching the footman viciously in the kidneys. He waited until Richards had stopped gasping and retching, and said calmly, 'I have only just begun. So, my good fellow, if you do not wish me to beat you to a pulp, you will tell me why you lured Miss Armitage into that morning room and professed to be in love with her.'

'I'll tell you, your grace,' gabbled Richards, 'only let me sit down.'

The duke nodded. 'Now,' he said, 'begin at the beginning.'

In a low voice, Richards proceeded to tell his tale of mad passion for Frederica, until he found his story violently interrupted.

He was a tall, strong man, but the duke jerked him out of the chair with terrifying ease and banged his head against the wall.

'Any last words before I kill you?' enquired the duke pleasantly.

'No!' screamed Richards. 'I've had enough. I'll tell you.'

The duke listened carefully to the tale of Mr Jackson and the gambling debts. 'He didn't say nothing about Lady James, that lady what found us,' said Richards. 'But he said a lady would surprise us, and as soon as I heard a woman's voice outside the door, I was to grab Miss Armitage. Oh, God, I've told you, and now he'll make me pay.'

'By the time I have finished with this Mr Jackson,' said the duke, 'he will not be in a position to collect any debts.'

He went back to Lady James's house and this time found her at home.

Overset by worry and guilt, Lady James blurted out, 'Oh, I am so sorry.'

'What about?'

'Why, the end of your engagement, of course.'

'And just how did *you* know my engagement was at an end?'

Lady James went red and then white. She wanted to lie, but found she could not. She was appalled at the enormity of what she had done. Fear clutched at her heart. She did not believe Guy Wentwater meant to leave Frederica alive. He would kill her, and then she, Lady James, would be embroiled in murder. She would never be free of him. She was deadly sure he would blackmail her until he had bled her white. Giles had struck Frederica very hard. She might have been killed then, but Guy Wentwater had not seemed to care. Lady James remembered Frederica's unconscious body, lying on the floor, her face white, her breathing shallow.

She covered her face with her hands and burst into tears.

'Is she alive?' asked the duke. It was no longer necessary to ask Lady James if she had played any part in Frederica's disappearance. Her sobs, her whole attitude, screamed guilt:

Lady James nodded dumbly.

'Then compose yourself and tell me where she is.' The whole plot came out, Lady James shivering

148

and shaking, her voice broken by sobs.

'I shall kill this Wentwater,' said the duke. 'Hume's mansion on the Richmond Road, you say? You will hear further from me, ma'am. What on earth made you party to such a vile plot?'

Calm now she had told her story, Lady James looked at him wearily. 'I don't expect you to understand,' she said. 'When I was your mistress, I was feted and courted and envied. When you terminated our affair, I took it philosophically. But then I began to notice how badly my reputation had fallen. I had had affairs before but had always been discreet. I flaunted my affair with you. I wanted respectability more than anything. I wanted to be your wife. I persuaded myself you might marry me if only Miss Armitage were out of the way. This Wentwater hates all the Armitages. He is not quite sane, I think.' She gave a harsh laugh. 'We made a good pair—he, mad with hate, and I, mad with jealousy.'

Despite her tears, she looked very beautiful and he felt an odd tug at his heart, until all his fears for Frederica's life came flooding back.

He turned on his heel and walked away. Lady James began to cry again.

*   *   *

'You must try not to be sick any more, Mary,' Frederica Armitage was saying. 'Goodness knows what filth that horrible woman put in your chocolate.'

'It is not my stummick any more,' whispered Mary through white lips. 'I'm that afraid. What if they kill us?

149

'If they were going to kill us,' said Frederica firmly, 'they would have done it right away.'

Mary shivered. 'It's harder to get rid o' bodies in the middle of London, miss, than it is here.'

'Oh, *Mary*,' said Frederica, exasperated. 'I refuse to be frightened.'

Neither of the girls knew where they were since they had been conveyed to the house, bound and blindfolded. They had been placed in their prison, a small room with barred windows at the top of some house.

A heavy, squat, mannish woman with a dirty apron and a red moustache had supplied them with food and water and had remained deaf to their pleas.

'You know, Mary,' went on Frederica, 'I don't know how it is, but I feel very well, despite a large lump on the back of my head. I feel, if we ever escape, I will never be frightened of anything or anyone again. I do not like London society. It *crushes* me so.'

'At least you can't marry the duke,' said Mary gloomily. 'That's why that James cat had us brought here.'

'I was a fool,' said Frederica bitterly. 'Pembury was so strange and withdrawn, he frightened me. I became my old self, just when I had begun to enjoy being brave. No doubt he thinks he's well out of it. Why did I never just *ask* the man what was up with him? I won't be able to unless I get us out of here.'

'We can't,' said Mary. 'There's men below keeping guard. I've heard them. And that horrible woman's built like a Smithfield bull.'

'Do not be so chicken-hearted. What would the Duke of Wellington have done in this situation, I wonder?'

'I don't care,' said Mary, beginning to sob. 'I ain't the Duke of Wellington.'

'Do be quiet,' snapped Frederica. 'It's all your fault,' she added unkindly. 'Why did you not think to tell me that Lady James had asked you to call?'

'Boo-hoo,' wailed Mary.

'Never mind. I am a beast. I am not angry with you, Mary. Here comes the bull with our food. Do not let her see you crying. Yes, on second thoughts, I will cry too. She must be made to think we are weak and helpless.'

When the jailer entered, both girls were howling dismally. She dumped the food down on the table with a grunt and went out, slamming and locking the door behind her.

'Now, see,' said Frederica, 'she has brought us bread and cheese which is very sustaining. But better still, she has brought us a stone pitcher of water. Do stop crying, Mary, and listen to me.

'That's better,' she said as Mary gulped and dried her eyes on the corner of her apron. 'What I want you to do is this. When that horrible woman comes back to take away the dishes, you must distract her, and I will hide behind the door, and when she comes into the room, I will hit her on the head with that pitcher.'

'You can't!' said Mary. 'She'll murder us.'

'Now, how can she when she is lying unconscious? You are not behaving at all like a correct lady's maid, Mary. I am ashamed of you.'

Being elected to the post of lady's maid had been the proudest moment of Mary's young life. Like a soldier being urged to serve his country, she stiffened her spine and said, 'I'll do as you say, miss.

I don't know what come over me, I'm sure.'

'Good girl,' said Frederica bracingly. 'Now, all we have to do is wait.'

Frederica did not have a watch and there was no clock in the room, which was simply furnished with two truckle beds and a table and two chairs. They had been locked up during the night. Food had been given them some hours ago which must have been meant as breakfast. Frederica guessed it must be around two in the afternoon. The fickle English weather which had been chilly had turned sunny and warm and the small room began to feel stuffy. Frederica tried to lift the window by reaching through the bars but it was stuck fast.

Then she stiffened, her head to one side, listening. 'She's coming,' whispered Frederica urgently.

'Oh, miss, what will I say? What will I do?' cried Mary.

'Hush! You'll think of something.'

Frederica picked up the pitcher and stood behind the door.

The heavy footsteps of their jailer came nearer and nearer.

The door swung open.

'Why don't you shave yer moustache, you ugly old cow,' jeered Mary from the other side of the room.

'Why, you strumpet,' raged the jailer, 'just wait till I get me hands on you.'

The woman advanced into the middle of the room. Frederica raised the pitcher and brought it down on her head with a crash. She gave a groan and slumped to the floor.

'What if she's dead?' whispered Mary.

'I don't care,' said Frederica, although she was white and shaken. 'Come along. We must escape.'

With Mary creeping behind her, Frederica edged her way silently down the stairs. Masculine voices came from below.

'Quietly now,' muttered Frederica. 'Slowly. We must go slowly.'

At last, they saw an empty hall below them. The voices were coming from a downstairs room but the door was closed.

'Stop clutching at my sleeve, Mary,' hissed Frederica. 'I will go ahead and quietly open the front door. When I signal to you, run quickly down and *don't make a sound.'*

Heart beating hard, Frederica moved silently across the hall. She gently turned the door knob and breathed a sigh of relief. It was unlocked. She opened the door wide, and then turned and waved Mary forward.

Mary saw the wide-open door and the sunny garden beyond. She hurtled down the stairs, missed her footing, and crashed headlong into the hall.

The door of the room where the guards were burst open just as Frederica was half turning back to help Mary. In a split second, she decided the best thing she could do was run to the nearest house and ask for aid.

She fled down the drive, hearing the sounds of pursuit behind her. To her dismay, the tall gates at the end of the drive were bolted and locked.

She veered to the left through the grounds, never once looking behind. She came to a low, broken part of the garden wall and scrambled over, ripping her gown in bramble bushes which grew thick on the other side.

Gasping for breath and feeling a pain in her side, she ran headlong across a meadow in the direction of the Richmond Road. She could see a carriage coming along it at great speed.

She stopped in her tracks and screamed as loudly as she could.

But that gave one of her pursuers the necessary time to catch up with her. He dived for her legs and brought her down.

'Now, you jade,' he growled, 'back you go and this time you'll be tied to your bed.'

He dragged her to her feet and twisted her arm painfully behind her back.

His companion was waiting for him at the break in the wall over which Frederica had escaped. 'Where's the other mort?' shouted the man, holding Frederica.

'Locked up an' cryin' fit to bust. Broke poor Mrs Cocker's skull, they did.'

'Wait till master hears o' this,' panted Frederica's captor.

'Look lively,' hissed the other guard. 'There's a gentry cove runnin' across the field. Knock her out so's she can't speak, and we'll say she's a madwoman.'

The guard twisted Frederica about and pulled back his fist.

A bullet whizzed over his head, and he stood where he was, his mouth open, and his fist still drawn back.

Pistol in one hand, the Duke of Pembury came striding up to them.

He took Frederica gently by the arm and pulled her away from her now unresisting captor. 'She's a madwoman, guv'nor,' pleaded the man.

154

'Turn your head away, Frederica,' said the duke gently. But Frederica watched and had the satisfaction of seeing the guard knocked unconscious. His companion made the mistake of coming to his rescue and was shortly flattened by the duke's punishing left.

'Oh, Robert,' sighed Frederica. 'I must be very bloodthirsty. I have never seen anything so magnificent.'

The duke came up to her, nursing his bleeding knuckles.

'What did you call me?'

'R-Robert.'

'Never did the sound of mine own name sound so glorious. I thought you were going to call me "your grace" for the rest of your life.'

'It's because you were *behaving* like a duke,' sniffed Frederica tearfully. 'So cold and formal, you terrified me.'

'What would you? I kissed you and *that* terrified you.'

''Twas the strength of my own feelings, Robert. I am not in the way of being kissed, you see.'

The duke came very close to her and looked down at her averted face, his black eyes burning. 'Perhaps I need practice,' said Frederica shyly.

He pulled her into his arms, his lips found hers, and he proceeded to give Miss Frederica Armitage a long and passionate lesson in the arts of love.

Out on the Richmond Road, Guy Wentwater dropped his telescope on to the floor of the carriage and cursed roundly. He would have just one more try to ruin one of the Arrnitages, and then he would flee to America.

'Robert,' murmured Frederica dizzily. 'Poor

155

Mary. We must rescue her.'

The guards on the ground began to stir. The duke started to unwind his cravat. 'I will just tie these fellows up, and then we can see to Mary. Then we must alert the authorities and see that Wentwater is put behind prison bars for the rest of his life.'

EPILOGUE

Emily Armitage was trying on a new gown in her bedroom at the Hall. It was made of metallic gauze, the very latest thing, and Emily considered it became her amazingly.

She had already been undressed and made ready for bed by her maid, but found she could not sleep. Papa was to drive her to Hopeminster in the morning to meet a certain Sir Andrew Jensen, who had expressed an interest in her.

Emily once more felt like the most beautiful girl in the county. Ever since that dreadful scene where Mr Wentwater had been discovered in bed with that slut, various gentlemen in the county had applied for her hand in marriage—and without even seeing her! Well, they must have seen her in Hopeminster and been so smitten with her charms that they had immediately thought of marriage. Emily did not know her rush of admirers was caused by her father, Sir Edwin, trebling her dowry and broadcasting that fact all over the county.

She had been too excited to sleep and had decided to get up and try on her new gown which had arrived from London only that day.

There came the sound of pebbles rattling against the glass of her window.

Emily opened the window and leaned out—and received another shower of pebbles full in the face.

'Who's there?' she screamed.

'*Hush.* It is I, Guy Wentwater.'

Emily went and fetched a candle and leaned out. She could dimly make out the whiteness of a face turned up towards her.

'What do you want?' she demanded.

'I must see you, my little love,' he pleaded.

Emily tossed her head. 'A fine one you are, coming around here after what you did with that . . .'

'Shhh!' he said desperately. '*Please*, Emily I must see you. I cannot be caught here. Come to the bridge at the River Blyne. I love you, Emily.'

Emily felt a surge of power. 'Very well,' she called, and then firmly closed the window.

Her heart was beating hard with excitement. She was a slayer of men. She was Cleopatra! She would meet him, and lead him on, just a little, and then spurn him. And *that* would serve him right for behaving like such a toad.

Guy Wentwater's plan was to persuade Emily to run away with him. He no longer had any intention of marrying her. He would take her to America and then get rid of her.

Soon, he saw her figure, wrapped in a long cloak, hurrying towards him.

'What a long-nosed frump she is,' he thought nastily, as the moonlight shone on Emily's face.

'You are a naughty man,' said Emily, giggling with excitement, 'and deserve to be punished.'

'I have been punished enough,' he said in a low voice. 'Sit beside me on this parapet and let me feast my eyes on your beauty.'

Emily sat beside him. 'What do you want?' she asked, throwing back the hood of her cloak so that he could get the full effect of the moonlight shining on her corkscrew ringlets.

'First, I must beg your forgiveness. That maid, Sarah, made me drunk and threw herself at me.'

'I don't want to talk about it,' said Emily, turning her head away.

'Look at me, dearest,' he said. 'Let me gaze on your beauty.'

Emily felt another great surge of power. She had kept on the new metallic gauze dress. She felt she held the destinies of men in her hands. She decided to punish him by flirting with him and driving him insane with passion.

She giggled. 'I don't believe a word you say, Mr Wentwater,' she said coquettishly, and gave him a playful jab in the ribs with her elbow. But so elated was Emily that the jab was more like a hearty shove. Guy Wentwater made a wild grab at the parapet to save himself, but he had been knocked off balance, and, with a startled cry, he fell backwards over the parapet.

There was a thud and a splash and then a long silence broken only by the sound of the rushing water under the bridge.

'Mr Wentwater!' cried Emily, leaning over the parapet. 'Oh, *Mr Wentwater!*'

A small white moon shone down on Guy Wentwater's upturned face. His head was propped up at an awkward angle against a large rock and the silver gurgling and rushing water poured over the rest of his body.

Emily, frightened, backed away from the bridge. 'I never saw him,' she said firmly as she walked home. 'I never, ever saw him. I never left the house.' And so, by repeating the words over and over again, she quite convinced herself of their truth, and when the news of Guy Wentwater's death was announced the next day, she was able to greet the news with a good show of composure, although she did hope it would not stop Papa from driving her over to Hopeminster to see her new beau.

*   *   *

Two weeks later, the small vicarage parlour was crammed to capacity. There were six Armitage sisters, the twin brothers, five husbands, one fiancé, the vicar, Lady Godolphin and the squire.

Once again the vicarage came to life as the sisters laughed and gossiped. There were flowers in all the rooms and the air was scented with perfumes, and rustled with the sound of silk and satin dresses.

The only person who was sad was Lady Godolphin. 'I feel old and useless,' she confided to Squire Radford as they sat together in the corner of the room. 'Colonel Brian won't come near me, even to discuss the end of our engagement. Folks say he's found another lady.'

The squire took her hand in his. 'Have you ever considered, Lady Godolphin,' he said in his high precise voice, 'that perhaps you made the poor colonel feel inadequate?'

'I! Why?'

'Your charm, your energy, your status in society. I fear the colonel is, *au fond,* a timid man.'

'Hey, I never thought of that,' said Lady Godolphin, brightening perceptibly. 'Damned if you ain't got the right o' it. Arthur always was as timid as a . . . as a . . .'

'Goose.'

'Why, you old charmer. It is a long time since anyone has called me that.'

'Quiet, dear lady. Minerva is about to make a toast.'

Minerva raised her glass. 'The health of Frederica,' she said, 'who has come through great peril, but is loved by the man of her choice, as she is loved by all of us. The news of her engagement to Pembury is the greatest . .

'No, it's not,' cried Annabelle, springing to her feet. 'I have great news. Drink a toast to *me. I* am going to have a baby!

A loud cheer went up and Mr Pettifor, entering with Sarah on his arm, blinked at the scene of noise and laughter.

'And *that* takes the attention away from us, my sweeting,' murmured the duke in Frederica's ear. 'Let us escape for a little. I have not been alone with you for a minute since that dreadful day.'

They slipped quietly from the room and sat side by side on the narrow steps of the hall.

'It seems very odd that you should love me, Robert,' said Frederica shyly.

'I love only you. I have never loved anyone before. I want to take you in my arms but I am frightened the strength of my passion will alarm you.'

Frederica looked at him with wide-eyed interest. 'I think I should very much like to be alarmed, Robert, if you please.'

Ten minutes later, Mrs Hammer, coming out of the kitchen with a tray of cakes, let out a squawk of outrage and bustled into the parlour, her face flaming.

She took the vicar aside. 'Master,' she whispered, 'there's Sodhim and Gommeral going on in the hall.'

161

'She means Sodom and Gomorrah,' said Lady Godolphin who had overheard Mrs Hammer.

'Dear me,' murmured the squire.

'It always baffles me,' said Lady Godolphin severely, 'how some folks always gets the words wrong!'